An Acquired Taste

CHERI RITZ

Other Bella Books by Cheri Ritz

Vacation People
Love's No Joke
Let the Beat Drop
Low Key Love

About The Author

Cheri Ritz loves a good romance, so writing some happily ever after to share with the world is a dream come true! She enjoys attending her sons' many activities, brushing up on pop culture trivia, and spending cozy weekends marathoning TV shows. She lives in a suburb of Pittsburgh, Pennsylvania with her wife, three sons, and the Sweetest Cat in the World.

An Acquired Taste

CHERI RITZ

BELLA
BOOKS
2023

Bella Books, Inc.
P.O. Box 10543
Tallahassee, FL 32302

Printed in the United States of America on acid-free paper.

First Edition - 2023

Editor: Cath Walker
Cover Designer: Sandy Knowles

ISBN: 978-1-64247-462-6

Acknowledgments

Thank you to Jessica and Linda Hill and all the fine folks at Bella Books. Thank you also to my editor, Cath Walker. In addition to the guidance you provided to whip this book into shape, you also helped me take the story to the next level. I appreciate you!

I have some awesome writer pals who also helped me along in the journey to bring Elle and Ashley's story to the world. Thank you to Karin Kallmaker, Stacy Lynn Miller, and Louise McBain for happily hopping on a Zoom for a title brainstorming session that resulted in *An Acquired Taste*. And also, a big thanks to Baxter Brown and Laina Villeneuve for beta reading. Love to you all for being generous with your time, knowledge, and positive vibes.

A special thank-you shout out to my nephew Hunter for giving me the full scoop on the ins and outs of YouTube—your notes proved invaluable while bringing the character of Benji to life.

I couldn't do this without the support of my family. I spend a lot of time writing in various places in my house, at various times of the day, and my family carries on like it's perfectly normal. I think they're getting used to this routine. Jaime and my boys—thank you! Hugs and kisses all around!

And to my readers—the biggest thank-you of all to you! Let's keep the stories flowing and the happily ever afters going.

For Jaime—my Star Baker

CHAPTER ONE

Elle Bissett sat on the wooden stool and slid the headphones around her neck before adjusting the mic in front of her. She'd done so many voice-over gigs in the past dozen years, the motions had all become second nature. She hitched her foot onto the bottom rung of the stool and waited for Steve, the show's director, to join her in the studio. Why she had to come all the way down here and read for the part she'd played for five successful seasons was beyond her. Yes, *Dog Tails* had been off the air for nearly ten years now, but with a reboot all hyped and ready for production she'd expected a script to be delivered to her home. She didn't think she would need to log any in-studio time until they were actually ready to record.

"I'm sure it's just a formality," her agent, Marigold Luxe, had told her on the phone earlier that week. "They asked that you come in for a face-to-face."

So there she sat, trying to remain calm and cool, waiting for some dude she hadn't seen in years to get this formality over with, when really she had a million other things she needed to be doing. She'd spent all morning going to get her hair done and picking out the perfect outfit for this face-to-face. Of course, in the end she'd gone with her standard: dark jeans, graphic T-shirt, and black blazer. Plus she'd promised her daughter she would take her swimsuit shopping since school had finished for the year. Now that Luci's freshman year was behind her she'd declared she was ready to level up her wardrobe for the summer, which probably translated to multiple bikinis and high-end label short shorts. Teenagers, right? But Elle knew it wouldn't be long before her daughter was off to college, leaving her home alone with no other purpose than her career. A career that had definitely seen better days.

Thank God the recording sessions of *Dog Tails* would be starting up again. Elle needed the distraction of steady work. She hadn't had a recurring voice-over gig in nearly a year. She had the bit parts Marigold booked to keep her busy, but if the bit parts dried up, then what? Commercials? Her mother, who'd managed her career until Marigold took over, insisted she avoid them, so she had. She needed to do *something* to get her career up and running again. This *Dog Tails* reboot couldn't have come at a better time.

"Elle! Hello. Thanks for coming in." Steve reached for a handshake, but Elle had been expecting a hug. The result was a very awkward dance composed of clashed greetings in which she ended up holding his hand in both of hers while he pecked her on the cheek. He cleared his throat before introducing the man who entered the studio with him. "You know Gavin James, right? He's stepping in as our casting director this time around."

Casting director? Hadn't the show been cast ten years ago?

"Oh, you're the guy I need to kiss up to then," Elle said in her high-pitched Fifi LaPooch voice. "Are we adding to the cast for the reboot?"

The men exchanged an uneasy glance.

"Yeah, Elle, that's kind of why we asked you to come in." Steve shoved his hands in his pockets and rocked back on his heels. "We're going to go in a different direction with Fifi this time around."

Elle's knees shook and she edged back onto the wooden stool. What was Steve saying? "Do you want me to change up her voice? Maybe it's gotten a little deeper with her age. Maybe the years haven't been kind to Fifi. Is she a chain smoker? Who's to say? I could do something like that."

"That's clever, Elle. Funny stuff. But it's funny you should mention age." Steve's gaze darted around the room, looking anywhere besides at Elle. Her stomach twisted. This couldn't be a good sign. "Gavin, do you want to tell her?"

Elle stood up and balled her fists on her hips. These two jackasses needed to get it together and spit it out fast. "Just tell me, Gavin. What the hell is going on?"

Gavin opened and shut his mouth twice without producing any words. Like a trouty-mouthed fish. He looked at Steve when he finally answered. "We've decided to go with a younger voice for Fifi in the reboot."

"A…younger voice. Okay, I got you." Elle blew out a breath. That ol' Hollywood go-to: younger. Sure she was zipping through her early thirties, but Elle knew she still looked good. She kept up a strict skin-care regimen, wore sunblock, worked out, and drank plenty of water. She'd always had a youthful glow about her. Hell, she'd auditioned to play high school students well into her twenties. On top of it all, Fifi LaPooch was A FUCKING CARTOON CHARACTER. They could draw her as young or old as they wanted to.

"Yes." Steve seemed to find his voice finally. He extended his arm toward the studio door, indicating that the meeting was over. The decision had been made. "But listen, if anything else pops up, I'm sure Gavin will keep you in mind."

"Yes. Um, please do." Elle's mind was sputtering responses as she reluctantly shuffled toward the exit. Was he really showing her out? Just like that? What bullshit. "I mean, I put a shit ton of money in your in your wallet as the voice of Fifi. I'm sure there's *something* I could bring to the table." She bit the inside of her cheek to stop herself from saying anything else. To keep from letting her anger bubble over in front of these men.

Everyone came to LA to chase their big dreams, but once you were inside the community it could feel very small. Everyone knew everyone. At least everyone who was anyone. Bridge burning was ill advised if you wanted to continue to work. How many times had her mother said that to her? It was especially true if you were holding on to the tatters of your career for dear life.

"Sure, sure." Steve's hand on her shoulder could have been a friendly gesture, but Elle was pretty sure he was shoving her out of the studio. "We'll call you if there's anything we think you could—"

He shut the door on her before he even finished the sentence.

Elle didn't look at a soul as she left the building. She needn't have worried—everyone was just as busy avoiding her. It was just so damn humiliating. They all knew she'd been replaced by someone younger, and most likely, cheaper. She'd walked into the building thinking this was a sure thing for her and now... *ugh*.

As she stepped outside into the sunlight, she tried to recall what Marigold had said when she told her about the meeting. *Just a formality*. Right. They'd formally kicked her off the show. Had Marigold actually said "formality," or had she done that thing where she'd said half a sentence then waved her hand in the air and let you fill in the rest? Seriously, if Marigold wasn't her best friend from childhood and good agents weren't so hard to find...

Still, Elle had been counting on this gig and the potential it had to get her name out into the world. Now she needed to find something else. Something that would get her out there again and jump-start her career.

She stabbed at her phone screen, unsurprised when Marigold didn't pick up. Mari would know to give Elle a little time to cool off after the *Dog Tails* news. Regardless, there was business to take care of, so she left her agent a message. "Dinner. My house. Tonight."

After bikini shopping with her daughter and a quick stop at the market, Elle settled herself in her favorite room in the house: her kitchen. She pulled up the show-tunes playlist on her phone and got to work. While the bacon cooked in the Dutch oven she chopped the carrots, minced the garlic, and sliced the baby portabella mushrooms By the time she was preparing the chicken to go in the pot, Luci had come Fosse-stepping into the kitchen in time with the "Overture" from *Chicago.*

Her beautiful, enthusiastic, surfer-girl daughter. Her mere presence brightened the room, even with Elle's lingering foul mood hanging in the air. Her long, poker-straight brown hair was drawn back in a loose ponytail, and big, expressive blue eyes flashed with laughter as she shook her jazz hands in time with the music. Her cut-off denim shorts and cropped T-shirt showed off the muscle developing on her skinny frame from the hours of swimming and surfing she'd put in over the past year. Newly sixteen, Luci managed to walk the line with charm and grace between sweet little girl and wannabe grown-up sarcastic teen, and Elle couldn't be prouder.

"Do I smell bacon?" Luci danced over to the stovetop. "Mom! Mom, are you making coq au vin?"

"Yep. Aunt Mari is coming for dinner." She swooshed Luci out of her way and added the veggies to the pot.

"Oh! Are we celebrating?"

"Possibly holding a wake," Elle mumbled.

"Mom!"

"She didn't get the reboot." Marigold appeared in the doorway. Her curly red hair bounced around her full face and her bright red lips hitched into an apologetic smirk.

Elle added the last of the ingredients into the Dutch oven before turning to face her best friend. "That's right. I just got the plain old regular boot. Right to the ass."

Marigold swooped through the kitchen, pausing only to kiss Luci on the top of the head on her way to the cabinet where Elle kept the wineglasses. She poured two glasses of red without missing a beat. "I'm sorry about that, honey. I thought maybe if you went in there and they saw your face it would snap him out of this cheap-ass decision." She leaned over Elle's shoulder to try to get a peek at dinner.

"Well, you were wrong." Elle swatted her away and clapped the lid on the pot. "They did not give one damn about my face. Hand me my wine and I'll think about forgiving you."

"You made coq au vin?"

"Yep."

"With those cute little pearl onions I like?"

"Yep." Elle sipped her wine. "Even though you sent me into the lion's den without so much as a heads-up."

Marigold hitched her hip up on one of the stools at the kitchen island. "Okay, are you done with that yet? It's the business. You know how it goes."

Elle took her time sliding the pot into the oven. It wasn't about going for a part that didn't work out. Marigold was right—she'd been there before. Many times. It wasn't even about being left out of the reboot. The truth was she just plain needed a job. Any job. Well, *almost* any job.

She brought the bottle of cabernet as she settled in across the counter from her best friend. "Yeah, I'm done." She topped up their glasses.

Luci looked up from her phone long enough to steal a sip of Marigold's wine. Elle shot her a warning glance which was met with an innocent raise of the eyebrows before her daughter turned her attention back to her phone. It was hard to believe in three years her little girl would be going off to college. Luci had big plans to either take the business world by storm someday or become a champion surfer. Either way, college came first. But once her baby flew the nest Elle would be all alone for the first time since…well, forever.

After a two-year battle with cancer, her own mother had passed away almost six months earlier, and the place still felt her absence. Hell, it probably always would. The three of them had lived there together in the home in which Elle grew up. Elle's father had died suddenly of a heart attack when she was only two, leaving her mother to raise her daughter alone, just like Elle was doing with Luci now. She wasn't ready to think about what she would do once Luci left home. She'd definitely need something else on which to focus. Some raison d'être. She was only thirty-three. She still had a lot of acting-career life in her, no matter what those *Dog Tails* dudes thought. A new direction was just the thing her career needed, and landing a solid acting gig seemed like a stepping stone to that path.

"I'm not really mad about *Dog Tails*." Elle sighed. "At least I'm not mad at you. That Steve, though, what an asshole."

Marigold made sympathetic sounds through a mouthful of wine.

"But, Mari," Elle continued, "you gotta find me *something*. There's gotta be a part out there that I'm perfect for. Just not—"

"I know, I know." Marigold held up a halting palm. "Not commercial work."

Luci snorted but kept her gaze trained on her phone.

"I don't need your opinion, Lu. I've been in the business. I know what I like and what will destroy my soul. Or at the very least make Grandma spin in her grave." Elle turned her attention to her best friend. "I need to get my face back out there. Give me something, please."

Marigold tapped one denim-blue-tipped fingernail against the side of her glass, silent for a moment as if grappling with a thought. "Okay, Elle, I might have *something* that would get your face on television, but it's kind of a reality type of thing."

"Reality television?" Elle groaned. Would she have to sing or eat gross things? Some type of celebrity death-match scenario? "Reality television is so ten years ago. I mean, who even does these shows anymore?"

"Mom." Luci looked up long enough to roll her eyes. "People who want to get their faces out there, obvs. Like you, DUH."

"The kid is right." Marigold shrugged. "Look, I need to check on a few things before I can set up a read for you, but if it works out it could be a good way to get you back in the game."

"Reality television?" Elle repeated before draining her glass.

"Don't say it like that." Marigold frowned. "It's not like that. This could be just the kind of thing you need. You'll be on TV with recurring potential. But, Eleanor, I swear if I pull these strings and get you on this, you'd better play nice or I'll have nothing to send you on but commercials."

A recurring part on television and all she had to do was promise to play nice? Absofuckinglutely. "I can do that. I'm in."

CHAPTER TWO

Ashley Castle wiped her hands on her apron and took the kind of deep, calming breath her personal yoga trainer would have advised her was necessary to blow her worries out. *Would have advised* if she hadn't had to let him go. Just the latest in a line of budget cuts the producers of her reality television show, *Queen of the Castle*, had rolled out.

All she had to do was finish making these chocolate chip cookies in front of the cameras, do one quick scene with her ex, and the season would be a wrap. In theory, it was a simple plan.

But for some reason when she went to the sink to soak the mixing bowl and turned on the faucet, the water merely trickled out instead of its usual robust flow.

"What the heck?" she muttered as she wiggled the lever, attempting to turn it on and off and on again. No dice. "Ugh."

"Hey, Ash!" David's voice was full of sunshine as he came in through the back door. His tone adjusted as he registered Ashley's frustration. "What's wrong?"

"There's something wrong with the sink."

"Let me have a look."

"Be my guest." Ashley stepped to the side so he could reach the lever, but she didn't have high hopes. David wasn't exactly the handyman type.

"Is the sprayer working?" he asked while simultaneously squeezing the sprayer.

"David!" Ashley squealed and put her hands up but not quick enough to completely shield herself from the water coming out of the perfectly functional sprayer.

"Oh, Ash," he laughed. "I'm so sorry. I guess it's working fine."

"I guess so." Ashley's wry tone didn't stop David's laughter. A typical theme on the show this season—she had somehow become the straight man to David's accidental cute-dude antics. Ironic—she had come out as definitely not-straight since their divorce. But she had no doubt the viewers would eat this up. She ignored the muffled laughter from the crew and tied a bibbed apron around herself hoping to avoid looking like a participant in a wet T-shirt contest. The network would definitely frown upon that. "What are you doing here anyway?"

"Oh, I can't find Slash's guitar. Do you think it's in the attic?"

These were the types of scenarios they'd been using all season to show the former couple interacting despite the fact their divorce had been finalized. David had moved out of the house three episodes in. It didn't seem to matter to the viewers, they still wanted to see them together.

"Could be." Ashley slid the baking sheets into the oven and bumped the door shut with her hip, doing her best to appear unflappable for the audience watching at home. Finally, the damn cookies were baking. "Go on up and have a look."

"Thanks, Ash." David flashed one of his Hallmark movie handsome heartthrob smiles at her before dashing out of the kitchen.

When the show started, *Queen of the Castle* was all about sweet moments between them. Ashley Castle and David Carlson, America's sweetheart couple from the hit teen drama *Canyon Rock High* all grown up and married in real life. David pursuing his rom-com leading-man roles. Ashley the doting wife managing their perfect home. It was a reality television dream scenario, and viewers ate it up. But now after four seasons and one shocking divorce, it seemed it was the chaotic moments that kept viewers coming back. According to the network people the viewers came to laugh at their missteps, much like the crew was doing now as Ashley dabbed at her soggy shirt with a dish towel while David went in search of a rock god's autographed guitar.

"Don't worry, I'll handle the sink," she called after him then gave an exaggerated shrug for the cameras.

"And that's a wrap for Ashley," James the director bellowed from the far corner of the room. "We'll grab that final shot of David out front looking all suave with his guitar ready to head out on location for his manly-man action film, and that will be the season."

Just like that the cameras stopped rolling and Ashley was officially on summer hiatus.

David jogged back into the kitchen. "Hey, Ash. Can we talk for a minute now that they're done filming in here?" Without waiting for a response, he put an arm around her waist and guided her into the camera-free space of the dining room.

"What's up?"

"Listen, Ash, I know you're hoping they'll renew us for another season, but maybe it's time to let it go. I don't mind the cameras following me around while I'm working, but my personal life…" He gave a shy shrug.

The plan for the show next season was to follow each of them as they moved on with their separate lives postdivorce— David the charming leading man, Ashley navigating life in LA as an out-and-proud lesbian. Although David had always been honest with Ashley about his feelings, he wasn't ready to come out publicly. He worried it would hinder his ability to get roles, and Ashley understood. The time had been right for her, but people needed to come out on their own terms and timeline. But still, she had an agenda that required keeping the show on the air.

"You can't quit on me now." She hated how desperate she sounded. She blew out a sigh. "I still need this."

"It's just that between the Hallmark stuff and this action flick, I'm gonna really have my hands full," David said as he grabbed her upper arm and gave it a gentle squeeze. The tender touch of a best friend. "Plus, the real fun of doing the show was doing it with you."

"I know." She felt the sting of tears at the back of her eyes. The same thought had taken up plenty of space in her brain lately, but she didn't second-guess their decision to end the marriage. She needed to be true to herself. It didn't mean she wouldn't miss hanging out with David though. The show connected them. "I'm just not ready to give it up."

"Okay. If they renew us I'll give it one more season." He smiled at her. Those bright blue eyes that melted hearts all across America shone with kindness. "But you *don't* need this, Ash. You can do whatever you want after *Queen of the Castle* ends. You just need to figure out what that is. In the meantime, I'm here for you—you know that, right?"

"I do."

They both laughed at the irony of her simple statement before David gave her a sweet peck on the cheek and headed out to film his last scene.

In her heart she knew David was right—her future was wide open now. But how to fill it, that was a whole other matter. She'd followed her mother's blueprint up until now by marrying a TV heartthrob. Ashley's father, though in his seventies, was just as much the handsome soap opera star now as he was back in the 80s. Her mother's entire existence was predicated on being the beautiful woman on his arm. A gig that worked fine for Belinda Castle, but for Ashley, it just felt a little…flat. She wanted more than a life as a high-society woman going from one charity luncheon or fashionable social event to the next. But what that "more" was exactly, she had yet to sort out. She'd have plenty of time to think on it while waiting for the network to decide the fate of her show. Heaven knew she'd need something to fill her days during the hiatus. Maybe it would be margaritas and romance novels poolside. That would be fun, right?

Ashley's thoughts were interrupted as her agent breezed in through the back door.

"They were filming David out front, so I figured I'd just slip around back," Jill said as she zipped straight to the fridge and helped herself to a bottle of Voss water. "Listen, Ash, we need to talk about your plans for the off-season."

Ashley balled up her apron and tossed it on the counter. So much for the summer of booze and books. "So it is an *off-season* and not a final wrap on the series?"

Jill sat at the breakfast bar and took a sip of water. "It's no secret that since you and David split viewership is on the decline. The network people seem to think viewers aren't getting that homey feel from you anymore. And they want that homey feel." Another sip. She was stalling. Choosing her words carefully. She was very good at what she did. That's why Jill Porter had been Ashley's agent from day one of her career as a preteen. "The network's still on the fence about renewing *Queen* for another season."

On the fence. That sounded pretty bleak. Sure, Ashley could get other acting gigs. Just shy of turning thirty, she could totally keep busy with Lifetime or Hallmark Channel movies. There were tons of those roles out there for her as long as her reputation wasn't tanked by the demise of *Queen of the Castle*. Plus, *Queen* was *her* show. She was appearing in people's living rooms every week sharing a piece of her real life with them. Well, maybe not her *real* life. The life on the show was a lot more polished than her actual day-to-day. But millions of people saw her face and her home and a life that was a reasonable facsimile of her real one, just with a tinge less chaos and a tad more home cooking. Her divorce from David had been heartbreaking, but if the show was canceled it would truly be the end of that chapter of her life. That was something she doubted she could handle.

The oven timer buzzed and Ashley pulled out the cookies. "You guys want some chocolate chippers?" she asked the crew who remained in the kitchen packing up cameras, lights and sound equipment.

The crewmembers all made polite but declining noises and seemed to focus even more on packing up. They'd all been around long enough to know that the food on set that was actually made by Ashley was not always suitable for consumption. At least not if you wanted something that tasted good. Or was certain to stay in your stomach. Any time they needed to show a delicious meal being consumed they filmed Ashley in the kitchen, but brought in prepared food.

Ashley turned back to Jill. "Maybe I do need to punch up my homey-feel skills."

"Yeah, you should probably just dump those in the bin." Jill cast a dubious glance at the misshapen and slightly burned cookies. "Do you need to check in with David before he leaves? I have a lead that we can talk about over dinner."

"We've already talked, it's fine." She shook her head. "I'll whip something up for us to eat. I think I have some eggs in the fridge."

"No need." Jill waved her phone. She knew all about Ashley's cooking too. "I'll order something."

"So, the way I see it, while you have this break you should find something to do that boosts your homemaker cred." Jill topped off their wineglasses. The readers perched on her head held her gray-streaked, shoulder-length, honey-blond hair off her face. Dressed in her usual casual-professional look—today it was slim-fit dark-blue jeans and a white button-down oxford shirt accented with several silver chains and bangle bracelets—few people would guess she was approaching her sixtieth birthday. Ashley often wondered how she herself had grown from child to woman over the years they'd worked together, but Jill still looked nearly the same age as the day they'd signed the agenting agreement. Jill was timeless like that. She recorked the bottle as she continued, "I got a call earlier today that could be that very thing."

Ashley popped one last bite of sushi into her mouth and waited for the other shoe to drop. Her favorite sushi, wine, and the chipper attitude about what to do on her summer break… it was too easy. Jill was the only agent she'd ever had, and she always did right by her, but she was holding something back. "I'm listening."

"How would you like to be on *Celebrity Cook Off*?" Jill shook her hands like sparkle fingers when she said it as if that would sell the idea. "They're building a really great cast, and you could be part of it."

"That would sound great if I could actually cook." Ashley laughed. "You saw what happened earlier. I couldn't even get a hungry camera crew to eat my chocolate chip cookies. And that was premade dough. All I did was literally scoop and heat."

"Okay, fair." Jill nodded and took another sip of wine. "But being on a cooking show would definitely highlight your homemaker side. And right now, if you want any chance of keeping your show afloat you have to show the network and the fans that you've still got it. You're still *Queen of the Castle*. With or without David."

Ashley sighed. Her show was in jeopardy and her summer schedule was wide open. Without a project to occupy her she would spend long days and potentially sleepless nights waiting for a decision on the fate of *Queen of the Castle* by the network higher-ups. It made sense that she should fill that time doing something that could have a positive influence on the fate of *Queen*. Even if it was a long shot. Plus, it wouldn't hurt to have her face on the television week after week to stay fresh in the minds of her fans. Still, there was the little detail that this was a cooking competition, and she couldn't cook to save her life.

"Jill, I think this is a good idea, but won't I need to actually cook?"

Her agent nodded, but to her credit her confident expression didn't waver. "Don't forget—this is television where anything can happen. They've made you look like Suzy Homemaker for years on *Queen of the Castle* with good ol' TV magic. We'll just summon up some of that."

"We cut the scene and bring in previously prepared prop food." Hadn't Jill been on the set dozens of times when the crew pulled that classic move? "I don't think that's going to fly on *Celebrity Cook Off*. They're going to expect me to *actually cook* the food. That's the whole idea behind the show. These people are trying to *actually cook* the best food."

"We'll get you cooking lessons. You'll fake it 'til you make it. We'll figure it out," Jill said with a dismissive wave of her hand. "You're an *actor*. You'll act."

It was a desperate, half-baked plan, but Ashley was desperate to save her show. *Queen of the Castle* was the only part of her life still standing. It had to be protected at all costs. "How does the show work? What exactly am I agreeing to?"

"The show will air for six weeks, each of those weeks has a theme—like Pasta Week—that will inform what dish the contestants must create. You'll know ahead of time what that theme is, so no stress there. They start with eight contestants, one leaves at the end of each episode until three remain for the final," Jill explained. "They'll film two episodes each week— Mondays and Wednesdays. They may bring you in for additional interviews on Fridays if necessary, but that's basically it."

Three weeks of filming in total, if Ashley could manage to stay in the competition. She would need to take advantage of any on-air interview time she was granted. Maximize any screen time her face got. With a little luck, by the time filming finished the network will have green-lighted renewal and they'll all be ready to get back to filming *Queen of the Castle*. Everything would be back to normal. Well, as normal as it was going to get. It would be fine. "Okay. I'll do it."

"Wonderful!" Jill's voice was overly cheerful as she refilled their wineglasses. "There's just one thing I should probably tell you about *Celebrity Cook Off*."

There it is. Ashley took a fortifying swallow of chardonnay and steeled herself for the catch. "I should have known. There's always something."

"It's not that bad," Jill insisted. "It's just that one of the other competitors is Elle Bissett. The producers are hoping to play off the old drama between the two of you."

"Oh, wow. Elle Bissett," Ashley mused.

"I know. I haven't thought about her in a long time. I'll never forget the way her mother Hélène marched into my office that day all worked up about Elle being cast as Bailey when she had a baby to take care of and…She needed to let off some steam.

Clearly I couldn't have done anything." She shook her head as if chasing away that dark memory. "Well, that was a long time ago. Will you be okay being on the set with her?"

Elle Bissett. A blast from Ashley's past. She of course knew to what Jill was referring. Ashley's role on *Canyon Rock High* was supposed to go to Elle Bissett, but she dropped out of the show at the last minute. Ashley stepped in and played opposite David and it had become the role that defined her. Hell, she'd married the guy in real life.

From what Ashley had heard Elle continued to work steadily, but always more behind the scenes. Voice-over work mostly. Ashley wouldn't go so far as to say there was "drama" between her and Elle. It had all happened before the days of celebrity Twitter wars. For the most part Ashley had just avoided Elle, which wasn't too hard to do since the fallen star seemed to lay low once she gave up the *Canyon Rock High* part.

Truth be told, Ashley had actually had a bit of a crush on the other girl back in the day. Before the whole *Canyon Rock High* thing, Elle had been on one of Ashley's favorite television shows, *Sugar and Spice*. Ashley was only thirteen at the time, and she tuned in religiously to watch Elle play one part of the duo of teen detectives. It was a ridiculous premise, but the show had been a hit. For Ashley a big part of her fascination with the program had been her attraction to the star.

"I'm okay with Elle Bissett." Ashley shrugged. "I haven't even seen her in over ten years. It won't be a problem." Who knew? It might even be fun.

"Great." Jill reached for her phone. "I'll make the call now and let them know you're in."

CHAPTER THREE

This is what it's come to. Elle pulled open the stainless-steel oven door and peeked inside. It was empty as she'd expected, but she was inspecting every inch of her *Celebrity Cook Off* workstation.

The producer, Kelly, stood at the front of the set rambling on with the orientation. Elle half listened while she surveyed her surroundings. Two lines of four workstations stood side by side all facing a long table on a raised platform where the judges would sit to taste the dishes and deliver their opinions. At the back of the workstations was an area built to look like an open-air market Elle assumed would be full of fresh ingredients for use during filming.

Six of the other seven contestants stood at their own stations taking it all in as well. Elle recognized most of them: Joan Brandy, the mom from one of her favorite 90s sitcoms in the back of Elle's line. Opposite Joan was Carina LaTraine, soap opera star. Michael What's-His-Name, the former NFL player was at the station directly behind Elle. Richard Bowser, host of one of those "shocking reveal" afternoon talk shows opposite him. The guy at the station in front of Elle with his early-forties dad bod stuffed in a royal blue tracksuit lifted his arms in raise the roof fashion. Elle vaguely recognized his scruffy bearded face from an old boy band, but which one she had no idea. Across from him was a young guy. A kid. Seriously, he could fit right in with her daughter's honors geometry class. She'd heard someone mention YouTube when he'd walked in. She'd have to ask Luci for the skinny on him. Always good to know who your competition was. The longer she outlasted her competitors, the longer her face stayed on the television. The more screen time she got, the greater the chance she would get picked up for some other project.

"Everyone comfortable with the lay of the land?" Kelly asked, drawing Elle's attention back to the task at hand. She was the one-woman welcoming committee giving them the grand tour. "You'll use the refrigerators and freezers on your own side of the set, but the community pantry area in the back is fair game for all. Yes, sometimes you will have to *share* items with your competition."

"No way, man. I'm in it to win it," said the boy-band guy.

The producer smiled and clapped her hands delightedly. She was a little too chipper for an early Friday morning, or any morning, really. "Mason, of course we want you to want to win, but we also like to stress that this is a friendly competition. Let's keep it light and happy. Speaking of light and happy, are you ready to meet the host of our show?"

Before anyone could answer, the quick click-clack of high heels at the back of the set made the whole cast turn. A gorgeous woman with big blue eyes and shiny pink lips waved well-manicured hands in the air as she rushed to the only workstation left. The one directly opposite Elle.

"Sorry, everyone," the blonde said as she positioned herself behind her counter and smoothed her floral print pleated dress with her hands. "I'm sorry I'm late."

She didn't really *look* sorry she was late. She didn't look like she was sorry much about anything. Everything about her, from her bright, long-lashed eyes to her hot pink toenails peeking out from her open-toed Jimmy Choos looked completely unrepentant. She stood with her back ramrod straight and beamed at the others, sweetly batting those beautiful eyes. Like they could officially begin now she had arrived.

Elle had never actually met the woman, but she sure as hell knew who she was: Ashley Castle.

Kelly cleared her throat. "As I was saying before Ms. Castle joined us, let's meet our host. You know him from his makeover show, *Dress Me Up, Freddie*. Say hello to our host, Freddie Simon."

Freddie came jogging onto the set, fashionably dressed in a bold-print shirt and linen jacket and greeted everybody before launching into a well-polished welcome speech.

Elle tuned him out, taking the time to study the woman at the station across from her. Ashley was taller than she would have guessed, but maybe that was the high heels. The only frame of reference Elle really had for the size of the woman was the five seasons she'd watched her on *Canyon Rock High*, and back then Ashley had been a teenager. Maybe she had grown taller since. Fucking *Canyon Rock High*. Elle had watched every last scene in which Ashley played Bailey Parker. She'd been kind of obsessed since Ashley had stolen that role right out from under her.

Ashley flicked her long, golden hair over her shoulder, her gaze locked intently on Freddie. The motion sent a puff of a scent—magnolia mixed with something fruity—wafting over to Elle's work area. What was that smell? And how could such a delicious, sweet scent possibly come from role-stealer Ashley Castle?

Elle had been offered the part of Bailey Parker first. *Exactly who we had in mind*, the casting director had said. But then overnight everything changed when Ashley's agent pitted her wholesome girl-next-door image against the message Elle would send to viewers as a teenage mom. It was a move right out of the dirty Hollywood playbook, and had cost Elle the role of a lifetime, and one that had been a sure thing.

Elle's stomach twisted at the memory and she shook her head to clear it. She blew out a deep breath hoping to blow that magnolia and whatever right back where it came from. She didn't need it clouding her brain and distracting her from the competition. Fortunately, Freddie Simon had wrapped up his welcome speech and the orientation was winding down.

Kelly took over again. "So that's it, ladies and gents, our goal is to shoot two episodes each week, six in all, so we should wrap easily within the month. We'll see you back here Monday morning. Eight o'clock sharp." She looked pointedly at Ashley.

In response, the bubbly blonde shrugged and slapped her palms on either side of her face. Macaulay Culkin *Home Alone* style. Like holding up production would be a total "Oopsie!" Was that how she viewed it when she took over the role of Bailey Parker?

Even though the other contestants were taking the chance to chitchat and make friends, Elle turned on the heel of her Doc Martens and strode off the set. She could compete against Ashley. She could even smile and be polite for the cameras. But there was no way in the world she and Ashley Castle were going to be *friends*.

"You're cooking for me again?" Marigold came into the kitchen through the back door from the garden. She parked a bottle of sangria on the island and went for glasses. "You are either very happy with me, or very unhappy with me. The suspense is killing me. How was set orientation at *Celebrity Cook Off*?"

"Perfect." Elle whisked the oil, mustard, and vinegar. A suitable outlet for her pissed-off energy. "I'm competing against Ashley Castle."

"Mmm." Marigold plucked a green bean from the plate and popped it in her mouth. She held up one finger to indicate she needed a moment to chew. Elle assembled the salads while she waited. "You made Niçoise salad! But you're not using anchovies, right? And did you get your hands on Niçoise olives?"

"I'm using tuna, not anchovies and of course no Niçoise olives since I haven't been to France in a hot minute." Elle plated the salads and slid a fork across the counter. Marigold was clearly ignoring her concern but they were going to talk it out. She owed her that much. "Did you hear the part about Ashley Castle? Her workstation is right opposite mine. I'm going to spend my summer standing ten feet away from the woman who stole the last decent television role I was offered."

Marigold paused, her fork hovering above her plate, and sighed. "Listen, Elle, I knew you wouldn't be happy about it, but Ashley Castle was part of the deal."

Part of the deal? Elle's mind reeled back to when Marigold first pitched *Celebrity Cook Off* to her. She didn't mention anything about Ashley. All she said was she had to check a few things before she could get Elle a read. Unless those few things were... "Oh my God. Mari, you knew Ashley was going to be on the show too? You set me up?"

"I didn't set you up. Drink your sangria."

Elle took a gulp of her wine, but it didn't help. She still wanted answers. "But you knew she'd be on the show from the start."

"Yes, I knew Ashley Castle would be on the show. The network wanted both of you. They think that your history could drum up some drama. And drama makes good reality television. They took that boy-band guy Mason because everyone knows he's a jerk and they figure he'll get into it with *someone*. That's just the way this works. Besides, you said you would take anything but commercials." Marigold shrugged. "So I made it happen."

Since Elle couldn't dispute that, the women ate their salads in silence. It was true—Marigold had done what Elle had asked her to do. Marigold was good like that. She made things happen. And the hard truth was Elle needed this shot, so she was just going to have to suck it up. She had a job to do. She was a professional. Ashley Castle was not going to cost her another job.

"There's not going to be any drama between us," Elle finally said between bites.

"Okay."

"I don't even know the woman."

"I know." Marigold's expression remained calm as she reached over and topped off each of their glasses. "Just go in there and do your thing. Be thankful your mother passed along her French traditions and taught you her professional chef skills because it's all going to pay off here. Cook your wonderful dishes and beat the pants off those other celebrities. Get your screen time. Maybe Ashley Castle will just turn out to be an acquired taste and things between the two of you will be fine. Or maybe not. Whatever. Screw Ashley Castle. You've got a cook-off to win."

"Damn right!" Elle raised her glass. Screw Ashley Castle was right.

"Mom. Mom!" Luci skipped into the kitchen. It wasn't the same kind of skipping from when she was a little girl. It was a little more sophisticated. A little more coordinated. Teenagery. Still a definite indicator that she was even more excited than usual. "Why didn't you tell me you met Benji Daniels today?"

Elle took another sip of wine while her daughter kissed Marigold on the cheek and slid onto the stool next to her. Who was this Benji Daniels, and why was he so important to know? Marigold's bemused shrug indicated she was coming up empty as well. "I didn't...who?"

Luci thrust her phone screen at her. Elle squinted at the video of a young guy grinning and eating s'mores. Lots of s'mores. "Benji Daniels!" The DUH was silent. "You know, on YouTube? He eats all kinds of stuff and sometimes a lot of it. He has like, a million subscribers."

"He eats stuff on YouTube? People spend their time watching him eat?" Elle didn't know about his YouTube activities, but as she stared at the kid she recognized him as the *Cook Off* competitor assigned to the workstation located diagonally from hers on set. "Of course. *That* Benji Daniels."

"He tweeted that he met Fifi LaPooch this morning," Luci continued, chattering excitedly despite Elle's eye roll. "He meant you!"

"Well, I've got some bad news for Benji," Elle quipped and pushed her half-finished salad aside. The dismissal from *Dog Tails* still stung. The youth of America knew her as the voice of Fifi LaPooch. Why the hell didn't the director of damn show see it that way?

Marigold shot her a warning look. "I thought we were moving forward."

"Oh yes. Moving forward." Elle nodded like a compliant stooge. "Me and my new friend Benji Daniels are ready to take the celebrity cooking world by storm."

"Mom!" Luci looked horrified as she helped herself to a cherry tomato from Elle's discarded salad. "No. Do not embarrass me in front of him. Just forget that I ever mentioned him. I mean it."

Why were teenagers so dramatic?

"It's okay." Marigold reached across the table and put a reassuring hand over Elle's. "You can buddy up to an old friend on set instead."

A snarky laugh bubbled out of Elle. "Ashley Castle is not an old friend. And we're not going to be friends." She sighed at Marigold's raised eyebrows. "But there's not going to be any drama between us either. Because I don't give a dippity damn about Ashley Castle."

"Oh, a dippity damn." Marigold nodded. "Now I know you mean it."

No drama. She repeated it in her mind so it would stick. *And definitely not friends.*

CHAPTER FOUR

Ashley pulled her custom-lilac Volvo SUV into the parking space and checked all her mirrors. No one was paying her one lick of attention and for once in her life that was exactly what she wanted.

But just to be safe, she put on the wide-brimmed floppy hat and oversized sunglasses from the passenger seat beside her. A glance at her phone confirmed she was late. She kept her head down as she made a beeline for the hotel across the street. She had specifically chosen the place because it was safely out of her neighborhood. To help the anonymity she'd forgone her trademark floral dress and instead worn light jeans and a navy T-shirt with a loose summer knit sweater over it. Simple, understated, nothing worth looking twice at. Incognito.

Just as they planned, she slipped in the back entrance of the building. Avoid the lobby and extra eyes. She hitched her plain brown leather handbag up on her shoulder. A mix of excitement and nervousness swirled in her belly. Not butterflies exactly. With all the secrets and stealth it could be bats. No. Too heavy.

And dark. Maybe hummingbirds. Her steps quickened as she pushed through the door.

The woman stood in the middle of the room with her brown hair pulled back in one long braid, a warm smile fixed on her face. She spread her arms to welcome Ashley, as if she wanted to make her feel comfortable there from minute one. Assure her it was perfectly fine for them to be there together. "I was starting to think you weren't going to come."

"I'm sorry I'm late, Chef Sarah." Ashley took in her surroundings. The stainless-steel equipment in the hotel's professional kitchen set a serious tone, tempered slightly by the delicious aromas of fresh ingredients and something savory simmering on the cooktop. "I appreciate you taking the time to help me."

Sarah handed her a clean white apron and led her to a workspace. "Jill told me about the situation and I'm happy to help." She leaned in conspiratorially and her voice dropped as she continued, "I have to admit, I've been a fan since you were on *Canyon Rock High*. I used to watch it with my daughter when she was a teenager."

This made sense. Sarah had the laugh lines and graying temples of someone in their late fifties. A little younger than Jill, but apparently a friend from way back when. Jill was very good at what she did and had wealth of connections. Ashley hadn't been the least bit surprised when she learned her agent had a friend who was a master chef willing to give her cooking lessons.

"Well, let's call this a mutual admiration, because I've come out to the Palisades Hotel several times purely for the cuisine here at Encore. Your reputation is second to none." Ashley could tell already she liked the chef. She knew Sarah was helping because of her connection to Jill, but the light in her eyes as she prepared the work surface for their lesson indicated that she was excited to teach. She was grateful for that—she knew she had much to learn.

"The first week's challenge is chili. Chili Week." Sarah pulled out a tray with a variety of peppers on it. Ashley didn't even know there were so many different varieties. Red, green, yellow, even purple. "The combination of peppers you select can make or break a chili. For our lesson tonight this is where we'll start. Now, I don't know exactly what peppers you will have access to on set, so I'm going to share a few of my favorite combinations that give that tantalizing mix of sweet and heat I think the judges will be looking for. You can do poblano with a New Mexico red, or maybe an ancho and a chipotle."

"These are all so fresh and so beautiful!" Ashley reached for a deep green pepper, but Sarah held her wrist before she could grab it.

"Not so fast." Her grip was firm, but her voice was gentle. "Before we do anything with chili peppers, we're going to glove up. Chili peppers contain oils that can burn your skin and even your eyes if you're not careful. So before we even think about doing anything with them we're going to put on rubber gloves."

Chili oils in her eyes did not sound like a road Ashley wanted to go down, so she did as instructed and pulled on the gloves. She listened intently as Sarah explained the steps to roast and peel the chilies.

"I've never been all that big on cooking," Ashley confessed. Hell, with the way she had to watch her figure for her television roles, she had never even been all that big on eating. "David and I almost always ordered in, and when we did prepare something at home he always did the heavy lifting. Even on the first season of *Queen of the Castle* that was sponsored by that meal kit company. Editing made it look like I was doing the work, but we actually had an intern put the meals together."

"You couldn't even assemble a meal kit?" Sarah laughed and squinted suspiciously at her. "That's pretty bad. I guess I have my work cut out for me here."

"I was terrible," Ashley admitted with a shrug. There was no sense in lying. Chef Sarah was here to help, not judge. "Once during filming I even managed to set off the smoke detectors while making pasta. And by making, I mean boiling the premade stuff from a box. The director had been mad as hell, but David and I laughed until we cried."

She and David had always been like that—best friends. It had been so easy for them to fall into that rhythm after working so closely together through their teenage years. They had been comfortable together. It had been great while it had lasted. Until they both realized there was no actual spark between them. No passion. Only a comfortable friendship. In truth, they were both coming to terms with their sexuality. Ashley was ready to come out, and David wasn't yet, but they were able to be open with each other about it. They loved each other enough to want more for the other. They just weren't in love with one another.

"It's a good thing I missed that episode." Sarah gave her a teasing wink. "I might not have been so quick to agree to these lessons."

"Chef Sarah, I promise you I am here to learn. I'm ready to discover my inner cook." She held up her rubber-gloved hand to indicate Scout's honor.

"I'm glad to hear that, because it's time to talk meat."

Although Ashley was no vegetarian, handling raw meat wasn't high up on the list of things she wanted to do. But if she wanted to show the *Queen of the Castle* fans she was a champion homemaker by winning *Celebrity Cook Off*, she was going to have to learn to cook. So raw meat it was. She twisted her lips into what she hoped was a confident smile. "Bring on the meat."

CHAPTER FIVE

Six hours. Elle was going to be making chili in that studio kitchen for the next six, long hours. On top of that, she would spend those six hours at the workstation opposite Ashley Castle. So far Elle had done a decent job of ignoring her. But there she was buzzing around like the original happy homemaker, wearing tight white denim capris that hugged her slim form and a flowing flower-print blouse that flattered her perky breasts. Not that Elle was looking. *Ugh.*

Since she'd managed to get her short ribs in the oven to braise, Elle had the big-rush part of the challenge behind her. As she moved on to dicing tomatoes and onions, she settled into a more relaxed pace. At his own workstation, Benji leaned his elbows on the counter, his face glued to his phone. A carefree smile flickered periodically as his finger scrolled along images on the screen. *Kids.*

"Hey, Teen Dream," she called across the aisle to him. "You know there's a competition going on here. Hop to it."

To her surprise, the kid put the phone down and turned his full attention to her. A good-natured expression graced his baby face. "My chili doesn't take six hours to make," he said simply.

"Is it the kind that comes out of a can?" she teased. Out of the corner of her eye she could see a camera man zeroing in on the exchange as if waiting to see if drama would abound at the Elle Bissett work area. But a little healthy trash talking was part of any good competition.

To his credit, the kid seemed to think so too. His smile widened to a full-on grin and he ambled over to her station. "No, ma'am. But don't knock that stuff 'til you try it. I ate two whole cans of the stuff on my chili dog episode. Obviously I lived to tell. And I'm sorry to offend your culinary sensibilities, but I have to admit, I even liked it."

He was a good sport and polite. Elle liked him. She could see why her daughter was fangirling. The kid had charm. "You didn't offend my *culinary sensibilities*, but if you call me ma'am again things could get ugly. It's just Elle."

He bobbed his head as he scooped a fistful of diced onion from her cutting board and shoved it in his mouth. It didn't stop him from talking. "You got it, ma'am, er, Elle."

The easy way he settled into her workspace reminded her of Luci. His lanky form leaning against the counter as he helped himself to her food and chattered away.

"I hope you've got some breath mints over there, kiddo."

"I really like raw onion," he mused as he continued to chew. "I should eat a whole one on my channel. Just like I'm eating an apple. People will go nuts! I'm gonna do it."

"I would recommend at least peeling off the skin first," Elle said with a chuckle. "You're a weird kid, Benji."

"And America loves me for it."

"Go make your chili."

Benji held up his hands in surrender and meandered back to his own space. Elle laughed and shook her head. He was odd, but he was a kid. Who knew why teenagers did half the things they did. They were just wired to be weird.

She now needed another onion and it was time to roast some chilies, so she grabbed a basket and headed to the back of the set where the fresh supplies were displayed. The common pantry. Before she could even eye up the selection of chilies, the telltale clickity-clack of high heels rushed up behind her.

"What looks good back here? I love this setup. It's like an artisanal market." Ashley Castle oozed enthusiasm. "Oh! And so many organic choices!"

"Yeah. Almost like hitting the Super Walmart." Elle didn't look up. Who the hell wore high heels to cook anyway? At least Ashley had traded her dress for capri pants. Grab ingredients and get out. No need for friendly small talk. Except Ashley didn't seem to get that memo.

"Are you using more than one kind of chili in your chili?" Ashley laughed nervously. "That's a funny thing to say, right? I mean…chili-chili." She paused and Elle glanced up just long enough to see her take a deep breath to compose herself. "I'd like to try a combination of two kinds. I'm just not sure which two to use."

Elle froze, her hand suspended above a mini bushel of jalapenos, then slowly spun to face the other woman. How could the happy homemaker be unsure about her chili recipe? Even seventeen-year-old Benji seemed to have a handle on cooking chili. "You're *unsure* about the defining ingredient in this simple dish? Isn't this supposed to be your thing? Cooking, hosting, making the world cozier for others?"

Ashley's expression went from quizzical to commanding as she straightened her spine. "Of course it's my thing. It's *totally* my thing." She waved at the display of produce in front of them. "There are just so many wonderful choices, I was thinking about changing things up."

The way Ashley chewed at her thumbnail while she considered her selection hinted that maybe she wasn't as confident as her straight back implied. Elle sighed. Maybe she shouldn't have snapped at her. This was supposed to be a friendly competition. The last thing she needed was for the camera people to think there was some sort of drama brewing here. She should try a little harder to have a camera-appropriate interaction. There had to be something about Ashley Castle that she didn't find completely off-putting. The sexy definition those high heels gave her calves was one. Elle blinked hard to clear her head. That wasn't exactly the kind of thing that would lead them to common ground in this case.

"Well, I'm going with the tried and true." Elle grabbed a handful of deep green peppers. "Jalapeno. I'm getting more creative with my meat choice. Braised short ribs."

Ashley arched an eyebrow at her and her blue eyes flashed with surprise. "Are we swapping secrets now?"

Elle felt a familiar flutter in her chest. Get it together. This woman is the competition. More than that, she's Ashley Castle. She glanced down at her Converse sneakers. Yep, her feet were firmly on the ground, but her world suddenly felt off-balance. She attempted to right it with some go-to snark. "That's not my secret ingredient or anything. Just a tip from me to you for the next time you want to want to change up your chili recipe."

"Don't worry. I have my own secret ingredient," Ashley retorted, then in a stage whisper, "it's lime."

"Okay, Castle." Elle didn't know why she suddenly felt so off-kilter, but she had a competition to get back to. She was losing time. She couldn't spend all day comparing recipes. "Chest your cards. You never know who is listening."

Ashley put a defiant hand on her hip. "Now you're supposed to tell me your secret ingredient. Come on. Tit for tat."

The word choice made Elle's gaze slide down to the open top buttons of Ashley's floral-print blouse. What was happening? She was eyeing up the competition? It was time to retreat. Ashley Castle pushed her out of her last television spot. She was not going to steal this one from her too. Elle wasn't going to give her recipe up that easily. "Nice try, Castle. I'm not telling you my secrets."

"So how did the competition play out? Who went home?" Marigold propped her feet up on the brick edge of the firepit in Elle's backyard and sipped her wine.

"You know I can't tell you that." Elle laughed. She had kicked her sneakers off when they sat down. The grass was cool and settling under her bare feet. Mari had waited until after dinner to stop by, but Elle was glad to have the company. It had been a hell of a day in the *Celebrity Cook Off* kitchen. The first day on set of any new show usually was. At least, that was how she remembered it. "I signed that thing. The disclosure. This first episode won't air for weeks, and then it's a weekly thing despite us filming them all ahead of time. I can't tell you what's going to happen. It will ruin the surprise."

"Don't give me that surprise crap." Marigold rolled her eyes. "I'm your agent. They don't mean me on that disclosure. Your secret's totally safe with me."

More secret talk. Elle's mind slid back to the memory of Ashley's unbuttoned blouse, and defined calves, and that magnolia and fruity perfume. What was with that? She gulped her wine. "Fine. I'll tell you. That soap opera lady Carina LaTraine went home. The judges said her beans tasted burnt and since her chili lacked any decent seasoning, that was the only thing creating any flavor in the dish at all. It was a mess. And it stunk up the whole kitchen."

The women shared a laugh and gazed into the flames.

"How was Ashley?"

"She smelled a lot better than Carina's chili." Elle smirked before realizing she just admitted to Marigold that she knew how Ashley Castle smelled. She really needed to get that woman and her delicious scent out of her head.

Fortunately she was spared further questioning on the subject as Luci came out into the yard slamming the screen door behind her.

"Mom. Mom!" She marched over to the firepit. A girl on a mission. "What happened with Benji Daniels?"

"I can't tell you that," Elle deadpanned. "I signed a disclosure."

Beside her Marigold hooted, but Luci didn't seem to get the joke.

"Mom. I'm serious. Why is there a picture of Benji Daniels with you on Insta like you're BFFs?"

"I've seen enough of reality television to know how this works." Elle shrugged. "You have to make alliances. I aligned with Benji."

Luci crossed her arms and pouted. "I asked you not to talk to him."

"Oh, and I invited him to our house for dinner on Thursday."

"Mom! I asked you not to talk to him and you *invite him to our home*? UGH!" She threw up her hands, spun on her heel, and stalked back into the house.

"He's a delightful young man and very polite!" Elle called after her daughter before erupting in laughter.

Marigold laughed along with her. "You didn't."

"I did." She swiped at the tears under her eyes. "He really is a nice kid and I thought he and Luci would get along."

"You aligned yourself with the YouTube star?" Marigold shook her head and her red curls danced. "You couldn't have picked on someone your own age?"

"I am nothing if not unpredictable."

"Yeah, well don't 'unpredictable' yourself out of a gig. Everyone on that show is playing the same game you are. They're all trying to win."

"Don't worry about me. I've seen my competition in action. I know what I'm up against now." Elle leaned back in her seat and kicked her feet up. "There's only one competitor that can keep up with me. And she's not gonna beat me this time."

CHAPTER SIX

Ashley squinted at her apple pie through the slim window in the hulking metal oven. Her chest swelled with pride. This was her second lesson with Chef Sarah, and they were both quite pleased with her progress. There was barely a difference between her creation and Sarah's beside it. "I seriously did it. I baked a pie."

"I knew you could." Sarah grinned. She had offered her pie-making instruction for the late afternoon, leaving her sous chef to handle the early-bird dinner orders. Ashley had promised she would make the most of their time together. "But you can't rush the process and staring won't make the magic happen any faster."

"I can't help it. They're getting so golden and beautiful," Ashley said as she put her arms out to her sides and spun across the floor to the flour-covered workspace. Since all the baking for the restaurant had been completed earlier in the day the women had the space to themselves. "You know, I just might pull this off."

"You did well with your chili yesterday, right?"

"Well, I'm not supposed to talk about it, but let's put it this way—there was only one other contestant who didn't use ground beef."

"Someone else used diced beef chuck?" Sarah looked impressed.

"No. Elle Bissett used braised short ribs and I have to admit, it was delicious. She really seemed to know her way around a kitchen, and as I recall from when we were kids, her mother was some kind of French chef back in the day. I have a feeling she's a pretty good cook."

Actually, Ashley had a lot of feelings about Elle Bissett and a bunch of them were stirred up during their produce discussion the day before. She'd had such a crush on Elle when she was a teenager. She'd thought discussing chili pepper choices might be a way to break the ice between them. Maybe even get her flirt on a little bit. But it had fallen flat. Apparently Elle still had a real chip on her shoulder when it came to Ashley, which wasn't fair at all. It wasn't Ashley's fault that Elle's personal business lost her the role on *Canyon Rock High*. If Ashley hadn't taken the part someone else would have. That was how the business worked. The fact that Elle seemed to be holding that against her after all these years was just absolutely…frustrating. Especially on top of those other feelings that had sprung up. The ones about how damn good Elle looked zipping around the kitchen in jeans that hugged her curves in all the right places. Or the way Elle's throaty laugh when she cracked jokes with the other competitors stirred a pleasant buzz in Ashley's midsection.

The ding of the timer announcing the pies done brought her back to the task at hand. "They're ready!"

Less than thirty minutes later, Ashley was pushing through the heavy back door of the hotel with her still-warm pie in a bakery box and her heart soaring with confidence. She was ready to face the *Celebrity Cook Off* pie challenge. It was amazing how much knowledge she absorbed from Chef Sarah. Not only that, she was really starting to enjoy her time in the kitchen. She should probably send Sarah some kind of thank-you. Wine, or flowers, or at least a handwritten note and a cute—

She stopped midstep when she spotted Elle Bissett at the end of the block, staring right at her. There was nowhere to hide. She was right there, outside Encore. And Elle had spotted her.

The women locked gazes and Ashley quickly assessed her options. She could duck back into the hotel. Or just turn and go the other way and pretend this never happened. Elle Bissett would never let her off the hook that easily and Ashley would only have to answer additional questions about running away. Most likely Elle wasn't going to give her the opportunity to make a quick escape anyway.

In what seemed like four giant strides Elle was toe to toe with Ashley, her gaze zeroed in on the bakery box. "That wouldn't happen to be…" She sniffed the air. "An apple pie in the box, would it?"

"No. I mean, yes." Ashley held up a free hand like she was halting traffic. *Do not let this woman throw you into a tailspin. You've done nothing wrong.* "It's not what you think."

Elle rocked back on the heels of her boots and crossed her arms. Her eyebrow cocked up quizzically. "You're not slinking out the back of a hotel into an alley with tomorrow's challenge already completed in your hand?"

"No!" Did Elle actually think she had purchased a pie she intended to pass off as one she made? She wasn't breaking any rules by taking cooking lessons. She wasn't *cheating*. "That's not what this is. I'm not *slinking*, and you've got no room to talk. You're in the alley behind the hotel too."

"Well, I'm in the alley because I was trying to lose some paparazzi. A pic or two is fine, but I don't need them following me all night. Five seasons of *Dog Tails* and no one paid me one lick of attention. One episode of a cooking competition in the can and suddenly I'm a hot topic. The show hasn't even aired. It doesn't make any sense." Elle's vintage black leather jacket bunched at the shoulders as she shrugged. She narrowed her eyes at the bakery box again. "So, what's with the pie?"

"I made it myself."

"You made a pie at a hotel?"

"Yes."

"And according to the *Cook Off* schedule, tomorrow's challenge is pie, so that's quite a coincidence. But also, you don't want anyone to know you were here, so you came out the back." Elle rubbed her chin like she was Sherlock Holmes putting the pieces of a great mystery together. "Oh my God. You're sleeping with a baker!"

"Don't be vulgar." Ashley pulled the box protectively against her chest. The last time they'd crossed paths Elle could barely be bothered to string two sentences together in conversation. Now they were joking about sex? "I am not sleeping with a baker. I just needed a little help with my pie-making technique, and the head chef at Encore offered to give me some pointers. She's very friendly and helpful like that."

"Were you really getting pie pointers?" The corner of Elle's mouth hitched up in a smirk. Was she making fun of her? And looking sexy while she did it? She was so damn infuriating. Maybe it was time to ask *her* some questions.

"Were you really ducking paparazzi?"

Elle bit her lip and nodded. Still sexy. "I really was. I was on my way to dinner at Encore with a date and—" Her gaze focused on something over Ashley's shoulder. Her expression sobered. "And there she is now."

Paparazzi outside Encore? While Ashley was taking cooking lessons there to boost her homemaker cred? This was a recipe for disaster. She twisted to see who Elle was talking about. "That skinny woman in the minidress? She's the paparazzi? She doesn't even have a camera."

"Are you coming or what?" the woman called. She posed with one hand balled on her hip, and inspected the manicure on the other, clearly annoyed with the delay. "I'm hungry."

Elle waved at the woman to indicate she was on her way. "Nope. That's my date. See you tomorrow, Castle. Enjoy your pie."

Elle's date was a woman. For some reason this pleased Ashley more than she cared to admit. She'd never really heard much scuttlebutt regarding Elle and dating—not recently anyway. So, now she knew—Elle dated women. *No reason to get worked up about it,* she reminded her heart. Elle was her competition in the *Cook Off* kitchen.

"Yeah, you too." *Damn it.* Why was she such a verbal mess around this woman? The last thing she meant to do was compare Elle's lady friend to pie. "Your date, I mean."

But Elle didn't seem to hear her. She was jogging down the block to meet her date. And suddenly Ashley wasn't quite as excited about her plans to go home and eat her apple pie.

Wednesday morning, Ashley arrived on set early hoping to have a quick word about the merits of discretion with Elle, or at the very least, beg her to keep her big mouth shut about their chance encounter outside of Encore. But as luck would have it, Elle breezed into the studio at the last possible moment. There was no time before filming for anything but a pitiful, pleading glance across the aisle between their workstations which Elle seemed to miss altogether.

Despite her zero-hour arrival, Elle appeared cool as a cucumber as she tied her *Celebrity Cook Off* apron around her waist and turned her attention to Freddie Simon, the host, as he recited the show's intro and announced the day's challenge. They were making pies. Blah, blah, blah. As he recorded a couple of takes, Ashley's mind wandered and she peeked over her shoulder to check out the competition. Elle was wearing her usual tight jeans and tennis shoes, although today's were a bright red pair that really drew the eye. How many pairs of sensible shoes did that woman own? And how could she be so full of energy first thing in the morning, bouncing on her toes like she was ready to spring into action? Maybe she'd hit the coffee extra hard that morning. Maybe Ashley should've done the same.

Ashley turned her attention back to her own cooking space and tried to run through her apple pie recipe in her mind.

Unfortunately, her brain was still shaking off the morning fog. She'd tossed and turned for a good portion of the night. When she returned home, she'd cut a slice of apple pie for herself and picked at it while she Skyped with Jill. It was bad enough that Elle knew why Ashley had been there, but the fact that the paparazzi had nearly caught her taking cooking lessons was enough to give Jill serious pause. There was just too much of a chance that Ashley would be spotted by the sneaky cameras and exposed as a cooking fraud. By the time they'd ended the call, Jill had pulled the plug on any more sessions with Chef Sarah, and Ashley had lost all the confidence she'd gained in her ability to cook well enough to stay on the show much longer. It was possible she'd eke by on Pie Week if she could muster up some energy and pull herself together, but after that she was pretty much a sitting duck. Even that teenager who ate weird stuff on the Internet was a better cook than she was.

"Are you just going to stand here all morning, or are you gonna start baking?" She hadn't noticed Elle enter her workstation. "Or are you going with option three and magically pulling a pie out of your sleeve?" Elle's wiggling eyebrows indicated she was teasing, but Ashley's tired stomach twisted with worry.

"I told you that was never my intention." Ashley's harsh whisper seemed to startle Elle, who took a big step back. *Pull yourself together.* Snapping at Elle was no way to convince her to keep the secret of their meeting the night before. "I'm sorry. I didn't mean to be sharp. I didn't sleep well last night."

"Well you were sharp. Very sharp. Downright pokey and pinchy." Elle seemed like she was teasing, but she retreated to her own workstation without pushing the conversation any further.

Ashley pulled out her mixing bowls and gathered the ingredients to make her crust. Sarah had taught her how to make a damn good apple pie. She had to focus on the task at hand. Get through this challenge and worry about the next one later. That was all she could do. Well, that and maybe some Internet research. Not quite the personal instruction she'd become accustomed to, but better than nothing. She went through the motions of using the pastry cutter to combine the butter with the other ingredients and did her best to shut out the idle chatter of the other contestants. As she clicked on the mixer to do its thing, she glanced up at Benji's station where he and Elle were laughing over his pie plans. A camera was there recording the entire exchange.

"I'm making a s'mores pie." Benji grinned. "I was inspired by that time I ate forty-seven s'mores. It was epic."

"I think using marshmallow on top is pure genius." Elle nodded. "But you know what would really take it to the next level? Use the torch to toast it. I think that would knock it out of the park."

"I get to use the kitchen blowtorch? That's killer!"

"Yeah, good thing we'll have it all on film," Elle quipped and gave him a light punch in the shoulder. "You know, for insurance purposes and stuff."

As Elle sauntered back to her own pie preparations, Ashley clicked off the mixer and calculated her next steps. She needed to get the crust rolled out and start on the filling. What she didn't need was to get sidetracked worrying about what Elle and Benji had been laughing about before they started talking pie. Had Elle gone over there originally to blab about Ashley's lessons? Would she do that to her? Ratting her out to a teenager seemed especially low, but if Elle really did hold a grudge against her from their own adolescence, who knew what she would do to knock her out of the competition? The kid said he had tens of thousands of subscribers. If he mentioned it on his YouTube channel it would be everywhere. Ashley rolled out the dough, taking care to keep its thickness even. The camera and boom were *right there* while they were talking. They would have heard every word Elle and Benji said. If her fans found out that a week ago she didn't even know how to make an apple pie, they would think she was a total fraud. They would turn on her. No fans, no *Queen of the Castle*.

She grabbed a basket and stalked over to the supply area to select apples. It would really suck if Elle sold her out. It wasn't fair. She couldn't just sit back and wait for it to happen. She filled her basket with Granny Smiths—the apple Sarah told her to go with—and straightened her spine to her full height. She made a damn good apple pie last night and she could make another one today. She would prove she deserved to stay in the competition. "It doesn't matter what *she* says about me."

"What who says about you?"

Ashley spun, Granny Smith still in hand, and came face-to-face with Elle. Of all the rotten luck. "I, uh…you heard that?"

"I'm sorry, were you talking to that apple and I interrupted?"

"No I was…" Ashley's breath hitched at the way Elle's smile quirked up on one side. Why did she have to look so sexy? Ashley was trying to stand up to her. She didn't need her knees going weak. It was just the remnants of a ridiculous teenage crush that she should be long over. "Look, Elle, let's just get this out in the open so we can get on with the competition. Are you planning on blabbing my secret to the world, or what?"

"Blabbing your…secret?"

Ashley leaned in closer. She could smell Elle's fresh, soapy scent and resisted the urge to brush a smudge of flour off her forehead. "About how I was taking cooking lessons because I don't know how to cook."

Elle bit her bottom lip and shook her head. "I didn't know you don't know how to cook."

"I told you last night I was getting instruction from the head chef at Encore and that's why I was carrying a pie out the back door."

"I thought you just needed a little help with your pie-making technique. I mean, that's what you said, so that's what I thought." She put her palm on her chest like she was grasping at pearls. "You can't cook?"

Ashley's gaze darted around the kitchen. Could anyone hear them? None of the cameras seemed to be following the exchange. Still, no need to tempt fate. "Please keep your voice down." Did this woman have no sense of discretion? She blew out a breath. Elle already knew the gist of the issue—there was no use pussyfooting around it now. Ashley had to be direct and honest. "The ratings on *Queen of the Castle* have been down, and the network thinks it's because my divorce tanked my homemaker cred with viewers. My agent thought doing this show would give me a little lift, but the thing is, I can't cook. So I was taking lessons. And I need to know you're not going to go around telling everyone because I really need this opportunity and that would be a really crappy thing for you to do."

The teasing glimmer in Elle's eyes dulled and her expression hardened. "Wow. I didn't even know, so I couldn't have told anyone even if I wanted to."

"It wasn't cheating, and it doesn't matter anyway because now that you know, and the paparazzi were sniffing around at Encore, my agent called the whole thing off. No more lessons. Anything I produce on the show after today is all me. I am completely on my own."

Ashley expected Elle's expression to shift to sympathetic, but her face didn't change. The look was still hard. Unmovable.

"Okay, I never said anything about you cheating, so there's that. Also, you thought I found out some information about you and I was going to use it to push you out of your television gig." Elle's eyes narrowed. It definitely wasn't sympathy. More like disdain. "Sounds familiar. I wonder why you would think someone would act that way?"

This wasn't what Ashley meant to do. She'd only wanted to be reassured that Elle wasn't laughing at her behind her back. She just wanted to know that Elle wasn't going to tell anyone and embarrass her in front of her fans. "I didn't mean…"

Elle held up a hand to stop her. "I know what you meant. I heard you loud and clear. Just so you know, I'm not going to tell a soul your business. That's not how I operate." She turned to walk away but stopped long enough to look back over her shoulder. "Good luck with that completely on your own thing, Castle."

Ashley's heart sunk. She'd definitely messed that up. Instead of finding an ally she'd stepped on the toes of an opponent. Suddenly she had a feeling she was going to need all the luck she could get.

CHAPTER SEVEN

"I've never had chicken cordon bleu before, but this is bangin'!" Benji swirled his finger through the remaining sauce on his plate and licked it clean. "Seriously."

Thursday night as planned, Elle's costar had joined her and Luci for dinner and he had turned out to be quite charming company, despite the finger licking. The three of them had made easy conversation while they enjoyed the meal, and Elle had a feeling this wouldn't be the last time Luci and Benji hung out. The two teens were definitely hitting it off.

"Any time my mom fries chicken it's the best." Luci grinned and passed a roll of paper towels to him for his hands. She'd been hanging on his every word all night and looking at him like he'd hung the moon, and Elle suspected her daughter forgave her for inviting the YouTube star to dinner. "That Dijon sauce is good for dipping potato chips in too. Should I grab some?"

"Easy you two." Elle stood and cleared their empty plates. "Save room for crème brûlée."

"I can't believe you own one of those kitchen blowtorch things." Benji pushed his shaggy blond hair out of his eyes and turned to Luci. "Your mom showed me how to use it on set the other day. Totally upped my pie game. You should've seen how professional it looked. The judges said that too—that it looked professional. Which was much better than what they said about Richard Bowser's pie before they gave him the boot." He laughed. "When Anthony said, 'Richard, I'm afraid your coconut cream pie has coconut cream *died*,' I almost lost it."

"Yeah, that was a zinger," Elle agreed. "He deserved it for that soggy bottom. But you know we're not supposed to go around announcing who got kicked off when, so zip it before you get in trouble."

"I will," he promised before turning back to Luci. "Seriously, your mom's peach bourbon pie blew us all out of the water anyway. She even served it with vanilla ice cream she made herself. It looked incredible, and I was lucky enough to get to eat a slice too."

"I know." Luci nodded. She would've agreed to anything Benji said, but Elle still appreciated the vote of confidence. "I keep telling her she should make an Insta account and show off her food, but she thinks it's silly."

"It *is* silly." Elle refilled everyone's water glasses and sat back down. "Why would people want to look at pictures of my food?"

"You wouldn't believe what people spend time looking at on the Internet." Benji laughed. "Almost eight thousand people watched that video of me eating a raw onion like an apple since I posted it Tuesday."

"That's a fair point." Apparently there was a whole online world Elle was missing out on. "But old dog here. New tricks are not for me."

"God, Mom, you're not *that* old."

"Thanks for that, baby."

Benji poked at his phone screen. "I think you should consider it. This pic Lu posted of dinner tonight already has fifty-six likes. And that's with minimal hashtags." He held out his phone to prove his point. "I can show you how to hashtag to really draw traffic if you want."

"*Lu?*" Elle bit back a smile. The YouTube kid had slid right into the comfort zone of their household.

"You follow me on Insta?" Luci was practically breathless at the revelation. She may have even forgotten her mother was present.

"I do now." Benji winked. Very comfortable. Maybe too comfortable. Time for Elle to remind everyone she was still in the room.

"Okay, okay. Just back it up a minute." She glanced at the phone. Her chicken cordon bleu did photograph well. "People like my food, eh?"

"I told you, Mom." Luci rolled her eyes. At least she was acknowledging Elle's presence again. "You could get a lot of attention if you had your own account. Generate some buzz, you know? I thought that was what you wanted. Like, the whole reason you went on *Celebrity Cook Off* in the first place."

"Wait, you're not on social media at all?" Benji's eyes nearly did that cartoon pop out of his head thing. Ah-roo-gah! "Give me your phone. I'll set you up."

Elle dug her phone out of her back pocket and passed it across the island, but Luci grabbed it out of Benji's hands.

"She's my mom. I'll do it."

"You're feisty." Benji's slow nod was dripping with approval. "I like it."

In a matter of moments, Luci had clicked and swiped and set up an account. Modern day child's play.

"Okay. We can take a picture of the crème brûlée and make that your first post." Luci slid the phone across the table. "Start off nice and flashy."

"Hashtag, lit!" Benji laughed and high-fived Luci.

"I don't know what either of those words mean."

"God, Mom." Luci rolled her eyes again. "You're thirty-three, not one hundred and three. You know what he means."

The app looked user-friendly enough, and she really could use all the publicity she could get. There were worse things she could do than slap a few photos and zingers on social media. Maybe the kiddos were on to something. Plus she had Luci for onsite tech assistance.

"All right, I'm in." Elle grabbed the culinary torch from the cabinet and set it on the island. "Let me get the custards and the sugar and we'll light 'em up."

But before she made it to the fridge, the doorbell rang.

"You expecting anyone else?" she asked her daughter.

"Maybe it's Aunt Mari."

"Please, she just walks right in. I don't think she even knows we have a doorbell," she called over her shoulder on her way to the door. She could see the unexpected visitor through the glass, and it wasn't her best friend.

It was Ashley Castle.

What the hell was she doing there and how the hell did she even get her address? Elle was having a nice evening with her daughter and Benji. She had no desire to go head-to-head with that woman again. Ashley had made it clear at the studio what kind of person she thought Elle was, and Elle didn't need to hear any more about it. They didn't need to talk. They didn't need to be friends. They could coexist on the set and just do the job they were there to do.

Unfortunately, there was no ignoring the bell and pretending she wasn't home since their gazes had met through the glass, so she took a deep breath and opened the door.

"We don't want any," she snarked instead of an actual greeting, completely prepared to slam the door in Ashley's face.

"Hi, Elle. I'm sorry to show up unannounced." Ashley tugged on the hem of her poppy-print peasant top. Once again, she didn't appear sorry. She looked very purposeful in her cropped white jeans, high heels, and red lipstick as bright as the flowers on her top. She had sexy, unapologetic lips for sure. "I need to talk to you about what happened between us yesterday."

"There's nothing between us, and we don't need to talk about it. It's fine. You do your thing, I'll do mine." Elle didn't bother to hold back her smirk. "May the best cook win."

Ashley winced, then blinked her long-lashed eyes several times. Did she not get it? Elle didn't want to rehash this crap. She had things to do. She had a dinner guest for fuck's sake. Sure, that guest was a teenager who was probably just as happy to have some time alone with Luci, but still. She didn't need to make things right with Ashley Castle.

"Elle, I was embarrassed that you knew the truth about my cooking skills, or lack thereof, I guess. And I was worried about having to own that in front of everyone. I was ashamed and that's on me. I just wanted to ask you to keep my secret. I didn't mean to imply that you would use that to beat me in the competition, and I didn't mean to insult you."

"You keep saying you didn't *mean to*, and yet you did." Elle shrugged. She'd made no move to let Ashley in the house. There was no reason to. They weren't doing this. "Are we done here?"

"You're right." Ashley took a step closer, making it clear she wasn't giving up. "I did those things and I'm very sorry. I've always admired you so much, and I was actually hoping that maybe we could be...friends?"

Friends? Elle nearly spat the word right back at her. Buddying up to Ashley Castle was just about the most—

"Mom!" Luci's scream from the kitchen stopped Elle's heated thoughts. "Fire!"

Elle forgot everything happening in the doorway and ran to her daughter. The roll of paper towels sitting on the butcher-block tabletop was burning and both teenagers were staring, jaws dropped as if frozen in shock. Luci was holding her arm against her body. Elle scrabbled for the fire extinguisher in the cabinet under the sink while Ashley, who had followed her into the room, attended to the kids.

"Honey, let me see your arm." Ashley's voice was calm and soothing. She checked out Luci's wrist while Elle sprayed the table with foam. "You were lucky—it doesn't look like you have much of a burn, but let's get this under some cold water. It will feel better."

"Oh my God, you're Bailey Parker!" Luci gasped.

"I was, but you can call me Ashley. Your mom and I are... coworkers."

In a matter of minutes, Elle had doused the flames and she and Benji got the charred remains of the paper towels into a garbage bag.

"I'm so sorry," he said as he tied up the bag. "We were just messing around and I was showing Luci how the torch works. This is all my fault. I didn't mean to actually set anything on fire."

Elle didn't miss the cocked eyebrow Ashley shot in her direction. Yeah, yeah. Teenagers were in the kitchen literally playing with fire. At least Luci seemed to be fine. The crisis had been averted and Ashley had helped. "Of course you didn't, Benji. It's all right. The important thing is everyone is okay." She caught Ashley's gaze. "It happened, but it's over. Let's forget about it."

Ashley turned her attention back to Luci's arm. "I'm sure it stings, but there's no blistering, just a little redness. You're going to be fine."

"Lu, take Benji into the living room and just chill out for a minute," Elle instructed. "Ashley and I will finish cleaning up and get the crème brûlée ready."

Elle waited a beat for the kids to leave before addressing Ashley. "Thank you for helping with, uh, all that. And for taking care of Luci."

"It was instinct." Ashley's smile was kind. There was a natural rosy hue to the apples of her cheeks that gave her a girl next door look. "Luci has Josh's eyes. She's a total blend of you two. It was so sad what happened to him."

Elle was always a little thrown off when someone mentioned Luci's father. The general public didn't even make the connection, for good reason. Elle wasn't ever actually involved with Josh Peterson. They'd been more of a one-night stand than an actual *thing*. But Ashley had been part of that pool of actors going after the same parts back then. That kind of gossip made the rounds. She nodded her agreement. "It was very sad."

Ashley inspected her manicure as the awkward silence spread between them. "I guess I should get going."

"Wait." Elle put a hand on Ashley's arm to stop her from walking out. Maybe spending a little time with Ashley Castle wouldn't be the worst thing in the world. Elle could at least offer a little hospitality after the way she had jumped in and helped. "Why don't you stay and have dessert? We have plenty and I promise I won't let Benji use the torch again." She quickly pulled her hand away when she realized Ashley's gaze was lingering on it.

Ashley bit her bottom lip as if still considering the choice, but then nodded. "Okay, I'll stay. Do you have another roll of paper towels? I'll help you clean this up."

The women made quick work of the mess, but despite their efforts there was nothing to be done about the charred wood top of the island.

Elle ran her hand over the damaged surface. Ugly, uneven scars. She sighed and traced a finger along one particularly dark ridge. "It's ruined. We've had this island forever. It's my work surface when I cook and our dinner table half the time too. We've gathered around it to blow out birthday candles, ring in New Years, and swap gossip since my parents bought this house over thirty years ago. I can't believe it's ruined."

Ashley tipped her head to inspect the tabletop then leaned closely, assessing the damage. "You know, you could sand and refinish the top and no one would ever know this burned part was here. Then it would still be your same island that stood for all your family memories, only refreshed."

"Home maintenance isn't really my thing. I could never do that." Elle shook her head. "It's a good idea though. Maybe I could hire someone to do it."

"You could totally do it yourself." She gave a shrug. "I mean, I could help you."

"You would help me?"

"Of course I would. That's what friends do."

There was that word again: *friends*. After the kindness Ashley had shown Luci, it felt a little more tolerable, but still she couldn't ask Ashley to take on this task and give up her time. Unless…

"Okay. You help me with the tabletop, and I'll help you with next Monday's food challenge. I'll teach you how to make stew." She nodded as if the decision was made. "Even Steven."

For the briefest moment, Ashley looked taken aback, but then her features softened and her beautiful lips shifted into an agreeable, bright red smile. "You have yourself a deal. Tomorrow we refinish the island. Saturday we cook." She reached out a hand to shake on it.

Elle grabbed her hand and pumped it once, but the touch felt so good she continued to hold on. She hadn't noticed before the flecks of silver that glimmered in Ashley's blue eyes. It wasn't until Luci and Benji returned that she loosened her grasp.

"Mom." Luci's voice was full of impatience. The kids had been promised crème brûlée after all.

Elle blinked hard to snap herself back into the moment. This was Ashley Castle she was getting hot and bothered about. Not gonna happen. Time to shift gears. "Who's ready for dessert?"

She opened the fridge and let the cool air waft over her. All she needed was a moment to compose herself and remember she was just making a deal with a coworker. Each helping the other out, nothing more. Also, maybe she should avoid touching Ashley from now on. Every time she did, it made her head feel a little dizzy, and also…pleasantly content. *Focus on serving dessert.* Somehow she doubted sugar-topped custard was going to quell her sudden craving.

CHAPTER EIGHT

"This has turned out absolutely beautiful," Ashley said as she wiped mineral oil across the newly refinished kitchen island. "I hope you're happy with it."

The natural grain of the wood really did go perfectly with the richly stained, solid-oak cabinets in the Craftsman-style kitchen. Ashley's main concern as they'd started the project was keeping the countertop in line with Elle's decor. From the moment she'd stepped into the room—even with the incendiary roll of paper towels—Ashley had been impressed with the touches of style, from the framed pictures clustered on the wall above the built-in booth in the far corner, to the oil-rubbed bronze hardware on the cabinets. Everything seemed to be selected purposefully. And everything just seemed so…Elle.

The women had completed every step of the project together starting with the trip to the home-improvement store for supplies, until the application of the oil they'd just finished. At first Ashley had been surprised at how Elle let her take the lead on the project. Even though Ashley was the one with the experience in tabletop refinishing, she'd been prepared for Elle to try to run the show. She just had one of those "boss lady" personalities. But right from the start Elle had deferred to Ashley and showed she could be the perfect apprentice. Before long they'd eased into a comfortable working rhythm of Ashley instructing and Elle assisting.

"I'm thrilled with the results. I can't believe we did this ourselves." Elle beamed with pride as she surveyed the final product. It was a far different expression from when they'd begun sanding down the charred surface. There had been a rough twenty minutes where Ashley was afraid her assistant was going to break down in tears. "I had no idea you had a talent for this kind of stuff. Why haven't they ever showcased these skills on *Queen of the Castle* instead of having you pretending to cook and host fancy meals?"

"Eh, I don't know. Jill always thought home-improvement projects were a little…déclassé. She didn't think we should go there. She knows what works for television, so I don't argue with her."

"Huh." Elle took the pencil out from behind her ear and twirled it absentmindedly between her fingers like a baton. "Anyway, I can't wait for Luci to see what we did here today."

"She's going to be impressed with her mama." Ashley tried to ignore the heat that was creeping into her cheeks and went back to wiping the wooden surface. Elle looked so adorable working that pencil. Plus, those were some damn strong fingers—an interesting new Elle factoid.

"What are you smiling about?" Elle demanded but she didn't stop twirling.

"Nothing. Just…I see you have a hidden talent as well. Are you secretly a drummer or something?"

"What?" Elle looked from Ashley to the pencil. "Oh, yeah. Habit. Not a drummer though. A baton twirler from way back."

"A baton twirler. Wow."

"Oh, come on. You were a child actor too. We all had to have some kind of 'special skill' on our résumé. I can't sing, and I can't really dance, so my mom enrolled me in baton twirling lessons and the rest is history." Elle set the pencil down and tipped her head to the side, regarding Ashley. "What was your résumé's 'special skill'?"

She'd walked right into that one. "Ah, tap dancing. Another child actor skill classic."

"Indeed!" Elle looked much more delighted by this news than she needed to. "I love tap dancing. What I wouldn't give to see you do the 'Shuffle Off to Buffalo.'"

"Ha, ha. I don't think so," she said, giving Elle a playful swat.

Elle laughed and grabbed Ashley's wrists to avoid the hit. "Nice try, Castle."

Laughter bubbled up from deep inside Ashley as she stepped backward trying to wiggle free, but instead somehow ended up pinned by Elle's hip against the kitchen counter. "I guess you think you're pretty clever."

"You know, I really do," Elle teased back and her warm breath puffed against Ashley's cheek.

She could smell the apple blossom scent of Elle's shampoo and Ashley's heart started to pound as she clocked the close proximity of their lips. What the hell was happening? Suddenly they both seemed to snap back to their senses. Elle released Ashley's wrists and took a step away as an awkwardness settled over them. Ashley's brain reached for something to say that would return them to normal.

"So, um, what happens now? With the table, I mean," Elle asked as she went back to gathering the last of the tools and depositing them in a plastic five-gallon bucket as if nothing had happened.

"We let the oil soak in and we have a drink." Ashley shrugged. Even though a part of her wanted to run from the house after whatever that was that had just happened between them, another part of her wanted to stick around to see if maybe there would be a repeat performance. "That's a totally legit part of home improvement."

"That's definitely my favorite part of home improvement." Elle laughed. "How about a beer? Let's go out on the back porch."

Minutes later, Ashley settled into the outdoor sofa on the stone patio and grabbed a bottle of beer from the bucket Elle had set on the wrought iron table in front of her. The matching chairs had been dragged to the far side of the large stone patio by a crumbling firepit and instead of retrieving one, Elle just plopped down beside her on the sofa. That first icy sip of beer was absolute heaven after an afternoon of sweaty work, and Ashley leaned back comfortably against the plush cushions.

"Should the firepit be our next project?" Ashley eyed the wayward pavers forming the broken circle.

Elle groaned. "Lu and her friends were shooting off some kind of bottle rocket back here using the firepit as a launchpad a couple weeks ago and things got a little out of control and it caught fire. In the process of us stomping and smothering it out, well, that happened." She gestured at the mess. "I need to clean it up, I know, but then our firepit will be gone."

"I was just kidding about our next project, but seriously, you know we could fix that. Or even redo it totally." Ashley could picture it—they could get much classier pavers and redo the whole thing. Total reno project. Functional and beautiful. It could actually be fun. "Also, you should really stop letting your daughter play with fire."

"Fair point," Elle laughed. "Listen, one project at a time. You just rescued my kitchen. I can't possibly ask you to rehab my backyard too."

Elle's backyard was charming and neat if not a little sparse on landscaping. A tall wooden fence provided plenty of privacy and the property was edged simply with greenery. One lone hot-pink tree was tucked into the farthest corner of the yard.

"Is that a crepe myrtle?" Ashley shaded her eyes against the bright late afternoon sun. "It's beautiful."

"We planted it last fall before my mother died. She used to love to sit out here in the sun. She had a whole collection of those big, floppy hats." Elle's wistful gaze landed on the colorful tree and she smirked. "I think she thought they made her look sophisticated and mysterious. Ridiculous things."

"I bet she was stunning in a floppy hat." Ashley remembered seeing Mrs. Bissett at the studio once or twice in the *Canyon Rock High* studio. She was tall with perfect posture and dressed to the nines. Classic beauty. Mrs. Bissett was friendly with Jill, and Ashley recalled thinking back then that all talent agents knew each other. "Is she the one who taught you to cook?"

"She was." Elle took a sip of beer. "And she was classically trained in France, so she really knew her stuff. She was always assigning me sous-chef duties in the kitchen. I thought it was just dumb chores. Meanwhile she passed on everything she knew about cooking to me. Now I try to do the same with Luci. And tomorrow, I'll do the same to you."

"You're going to teach me everything you know?"

"Well, not everything." Elle's lips turned up in a crooked grin and her eyes twinkled with teasing. "A girl's gotta have a couple secrets."

"We need to give your kitchen island time to heal, so tomorrow my kitchen is your kitchen. What will we be making?"

"I thought we'd go with boeuf bourguignon."

"Bourguignon? Sounds fancy."

"Don't worry, my little protégé." Elle patted her on the knee. "It's just stew."

The touch was soft and warm, and Ashley wished Elle's hand had lingered a bit longer. Warmth buzzed into her chest and up her neck. She was probably still just overheated from the afternoon's labors. She pressed her beer bottle to her forehead to cool off. "I hope I don't let you down."

"I have the utmost faith in you." Elle's lips brushed the mouth of her beer bottle as she spoke and Ashley felt another stirring in her belly. "Seriously though. You can't cook at all?"

"Seriously," Ashley confirmed with a stiff nod. "Not a bit. Thanks to my dad's soap-opera career, my parents always had a cook in our house when I was growing up. My mom didn't even cook much less pass on any skills to me. And once I was married to David and we had our own home, he did the cooking any time we actually ate a meal in. I know nothing except what

I learned from Chef Sarah at Encore before that plan was shut down. Damn paparazzi. They ruined everything."

"Not for me." Elle shrugged. "My date was very impressed."

Ashley's stomach balled with something that felt a lot like… jealousy. What did she care if Elle had a date and it went well? They were hardly even friends and certainly not anything more, despite that brief moment of playfulness in the kitchen earlier. "I'm glad it went well. She seemed very…sweet."

Elle laughed and choked on her beer. "She was definitely not sweet, and the date didn't go all that well. She spent half the night talking about herself and the other half talking about her ex. The paparazzi's interest seemed to be the only thing she liked about me. Honestly, I hardly ever go on dates. It's always been too tricky to fit it all in—taking care of my mom all those years, raising Luci, hustling to keep my career afloat. And then on those rare occasions I do, like the other night, something just always feels…off. Dating is such a freaking crapshoot."

Ashley took another swallow of beer to hide the smile she felt rising on her lips. "That's too bad. About your date, I mean. You know, it was the *Cook Off* people who had the paparazzi on us in the first place."

"I wondered how I got so popular all of the sudden." Elle smiled. "It was a good rush while it lasted."

"I couldn't believe it when Jill told me. I guess the producers are trying to drum up any interest in us contestants that they can. Any publicity is good publicity and all that." Ashley sighed dramatically. "Of course, now you're stuck teaching me to cook."

"Not stuck." Elle placed her hand on top of Ashley's. "We had a deal, remember? You helped me. I'll help you."

This time she didn't pull away and the women shared a smile. For as prickly as Elle's sense of humor could be, her touch was soft as velvet. What would it be like to have those hands run over more than just her hand or knee? Ashley shifted on the cushion, careful not to break the contact. The women had finally found a balance after their rocky reunion the week before. She didn't want to break the spell. "You know how I ended up on *Celebrity Cook Off*, but how about you?"

"I like to cook." Elle shrugged. Her normally tough façade fell and was replaced by chagrin. "And I need the face time on television to help me get back in the game. My agent, Marigold—who has thoroughly enjoyed many meals in my kitchen—figured the show would be a good fit for me."

"What about the *Dog Tails* reboot I keep hearing about?" Ashley squeezed her eyes shut, embarrassed as she realized her mistake. *Dog Tails* was a cartoon. "Oh my God, that was so stupid. That's your voice on television, but that's not your face. Sorry."

The women both laughed at the ridiculousness of her blunder.

Elle sat her empty beer bottle on the table. "Actually, the reboot fell through."

"That's too bad. Everybody loves that show."

"I misspoke." Elle held up her hand as if pledging to tell the truth. "The reboot is just fine. My part in it fell through. They're going in a 'different direction' for Fifi LaPooch."

"You're kidding me!" Ashley covered her gaping mouth with her hand. Losing that part must've been a real blow to the ego. Elle gave life to that character. Her voice defined Fifi. No wonder Elle had been so sensitive about losing a show. "No one else could give LaPooch voice like you did."

"You're very kind, but apparently someone who works for less will." Elle shook her head. "I'm sorry. I don't mean to be a downer. Here's the truth: for years I raised my daughter and took care of my mother, and now my mother's gone and in a couple years Luci will be off to school, and it will just be me. I'm on *Celebrity Cook Off* to try to drum up some interest so that maybe when I'm all alone I'll at least have work to cling to."

Funny, for as radiant as Elle was normally with all her confidence and sass, she was equally beautiful raw like this— confessing her truth. Ashley's heart went out to her. She could understand the heartbreak of a show "going in another direction." Hell, *Queen of the Castle* might be going in the direction of off the air altogether.

She and Elle, they weren't so different. They both just wanted to keep their careers chugging along, no matter what it took. She instinctively reached up and tucked an unruly lock of Elle's chestnut hair behind her ear. Their gazes locked and a gentle smile graced Elle's lips. Suddenly it was like an invisible force was drawing them closer. Ashley closed her eyes, expecting their lips to finally make delicious contact.

"Mom. Mom!"

Ashley's eyes snapped back open to see Luci coming out onto the patio from the house. She immediately sat straight up and finished the last of her beer as if that was what she'd been doing all along.

Elle winced. "Honey, we have got to work on your inside voice. You are sixteen years old. How did you not develop this skill?"

"Mom, we're outside. So my outside voice is appropriate." The teenager shrugged. "Anyway, I just wanted to let you know I'm home. And the island looks awesome."

"Thank you, dear." The easy smile returned to Elle's face. "Ashley deserves the accolades."

Was that the first time Elle had referred to her by her first name? Ashley fixed her face into a humble smile while she racked her brain for any other time, but she came up empty. First it felt like they were going to kiss, and now Elle was using her actual name? What the hell was going on?

"It's awesome," Luci repeated in Ashley's direction this time.

"I'm glad you like it." Ashley had worried that the new countertop would be a constant reminder to Luci of the fire, but she seemed unaffected.

As quickly as Luci had popped out on the patio, she disappeared back into the house, leaving the women alone once more. The moment they'd shared was gone though. Ashley chewed the inside of her cheek for only a few beats before she couldn't stand the awkward silence that had settled between them.

"So stew tomorrow then." She stood and stretched her arms to her sides. She would certainly feel the effects of the day's manual labor in the morning.

"You're leaving now?" Elle stood too, her brow furrowed as if confused by the shift in mood.

"Yeah. You've seen enough of me today and you still have to see me tomorrow. You'll be sick of my face by the end of the weekend." Ashley tried to laugh, but her heart wasn't on board with the joke. Based on the way her chest was buzzing she would be counting down the minutes until they were together again, but no need to clue Elle into that. She needed tomorrow's cooking lesson. She couldn't afford to scare her off again.

Elle led her through the house to the front door where they confirmed times for the next day. She leaned against the doorframe and eyed her up and down. Maybe Ashley hadn't been the only one who felt that vibe between them earlier. "Hey, I really appreciate your help today. I could've never done that without you."

"You're welcome, but you could have." Ashley threw caution to the wind and winked. "You'll make it up to me tomorrow anyway. Tit for tat, right?"

She headed to her car without a glance backward to see how her words hit. She would just enjoy the delicious anticipation until they met again.

CHAPTER NINE

When Ashley had left the night before, Elle and Luci had popped some popcorn and settled on the couch for a *Queen of the Castle* marathon. Elle had never really watched the show, but Luci was able to give her a complete rundown of who was who and fill in any blanks in the timeline. Luci had insisted on watching episodes from the first season because she liked how Ashley was all flustered and funny. Luci was right about that, but somehow Ashley still managed to look absolutely gorgeous anyway. *Well, of course she did.* She had a hair and makeup person, and probably a couple of interns pitching in around the house. And, clearly, she didn't do any of the actual cooking like she pretended on the show. Elle knew too much about what was in the secret sauce of *Queen of the Castle* to fall for the TV magic, but she enjoyed the program nonetheless. It was brave of Ashley to put her real life—or even some semblance of it—out there like that.

Now working in the same kitchen where she watched Ashley and David navigate the twists and turns of their daily lives, it all felt a little surreal.

She'd watched enough of the show to expect the elegant décor of Ashley's home, but what she didn't expect was the cozy comfortable feeling she got from the minute she stepped through the door. While the house was neat and styled, it was definitely lived in. The framed black-and-white photos of family and friends in the living room were candid shots, not stuffy posed ones, and the giant throw pillows on the couch looked perfect for a night of snuggling up and watching movies. Elle's impression of the house was much like how she was coming to think of Ashley—there was more there than first met the eye.

The kitchen had been a whole other delight. Granite countertops made an elegant and spacious work surface. And the space was loaded top to bottom with every utensil and gadget one could possibly need or want. No doubt all there to lend credibility to Ashley's cooking skills.

Elle was pleased with the way the cooking lesson had gone so far. Despite zipping around the kitchen in espadrille wedge sandals, Ashley had managed every task assigned to her with aplomb. Elle instructed and Ashley followed, like a well-choreographed dance, and together they'd assembled the ingredients needed to make their dinner a real show stopper.

After they got the brisket, carrots, and broth combination into the oven, the women had about an hour to kill before the dish needed their attention again, so Elle suggested they finish off the bottle of pinot noir.

The women sat side by side on Ashley's white living room sofa and Elle poured the wine while Ashley toed off her espadrilles and propped her legs up on the coffee table. It was like being at home allowed her the luxury of wearing sturdier wedge heels as opposed to her usual full-octane stilettos. Ah, the comforts of home.

"God, it feels good to get off my feet." Ashley sighed and accepted the glass of pinot.

"Why on earth were you wearing those shoes to cook in your own damn kitchen?" Elle settled into the cushions, careful not to spill red wine on the pristine white fabric. "We need to get you some comfortable footwear if you're serious about doing this right."

"Comfortable footwear is your secret to a good boeuf bourguignon?"

"Comfortable footwear is my secret to a good everything," Elle laughed. "Believe me, you need to get some."

"I wish." Ashley shook her head and her blond hair danced around her frowning face. "My viewers expect me to dress a certain way. The heels are part of it."

Elle made a show of comedically scanning the room, sitting up in her seat and jerking her head one direction then another as if seeking out a hidden camera. "Are we on camera right now?"

"No, silly." Ashley laughed and her eyes sparkled as she grabbed Elle's arm to pull her back down on the couch. The sound caused a stirring of wild butterflies to erupt in Elle's belly. She liked making Ashley laugh. "You know what I mean. This style is part of my *brand*."

"Maybe it's time to shake your brand up."

"No." Ashley shook her head defiantly. "You don't mess with something that works. Viewers don't like change. I've learned that from experience."

"You can still be stylish in comfortable shoes. The two things are not mutually exclusive, you know. Look at Reese Witherspoon. She's the picture of style and she's almost always in comfortable footwear."

"Oh my God! You're friends with Reese Witherspoon?"

"What? No! I've never even met her." Elle ignored Ashley's confused look and took a long sip of her wine.

"Then how do you know what kind of shoes she wears?" Ashley pushed, giving her a playful punch in the thigh. Elle squirmed like she was trying to get away, but she didn't want to get away at all. She wanted Ashley to keep touching her. "Well?"

"Stop hitting me. I don't want to spill wine on your couch and you're making me wiggle." Elle couldn't hold back her smile any longer. It felt so natural to be teasing and joking with Ashley. It was hard to believe that a week ago they didn't even really know one another. "I follow her on Instagram. Her outfits are always fabulous, and her shoes often appear comfortable. 'Sensible' doesn't have to mean trainers in these modern times."

"Okay, okay. You've made your point. I'm sure I'll find something I can live with." Ashley surrendered with a sigh. "I'll get online tomorrow and investigate options. Anyway, what are you doing on Instagram?"

"My daughter just got me into it the other day. Well, her and Benji. That kid is all about the social media." Elle drained her glass and reached forward to refill it, taking care again not to spill on the couch. "What are you doing with a white couch in your living room? Aren't you a nervous wreck around it? I mean, we're drinking red wine on it. It's a disaster waiting to happen."

Ashley fixed her lips into a straight line and flicked a carefree wrist. "*Queen of the Castle* production has replaced our white couch twice. This is actually our third one. You wouldn't believe some of the things we've had to have cleaned around here thanks to David's shenanigans."

The women shared another laugh. Clearly Ashley's home had been professionally decorated, and apparently professionally cleaned, but there were plenty of signs that it was lived in. Like the white basket in the corner filled with magazines, and the numerous romance novels on the bookshelves. Under the big front window there were two taupe fluffy bean bag chairs that Elle couldn't quite picture Ashley sitting in, but they looked stylish yet comfy nonetheless.

"So David is off on location filming his latest flick, all footloose and fancy free, while you're here left to worry about the fate of *Queen of the Castle*? Feels a little rude. I mean, it's his show too."

Ashley took a long drink of wine and her eyebrows pinched together. Elle hated that she'd put that look on her face. After a hard swallow, she finally answered. "In fairness, David can do whatever he wants. He doesn't need my approval. Well, not anymore. But you're right—thank God I have *Cook Off* to distract me. Otherwise I don't know what I'd be doing with myself."

Elle bit back the glib remark containing suggestions like max out on Netflix, catch up on her dating life, or get some damn sleep. Instead of an insensitive throwaway comment, she nodded sympathetically. "I can understand that."

"Really, David and I have remained best friends, despite the divorce. That's one of the things on *Queen* that is actual reality. So, I'm glad he's having success with his film career." The wisps of hair framing her face lifted with the resigned breath she blew out. "And truthfully, I need to use the time to do everything I can to save *Queen of the Castle*."

"Do you really think they're gonna cancel the show?"

"Jill says the network is *on the fence* about renewal." Ashley uncrossed and recrossed her legs like the subject made her physically uncomfortable. "Viewership has dropped since David and I split. Apparently single people don't track as homey with reality television viewers."

Elle nearly choked on her wine. "That is total bullshit. I've been single my whole life and my house is as homey as they come. Please. You've been there. You know."

"I do know that about you," Ashley confirmed. "But I'm the complete opposite. I went straight from my parents' house to living with David. I've never been on my own. I was part of a couple my whole life, or at least, that's the way it felt. David and I met when I was sixteen years old. He was my best friend. I mean, he still is my best friend. I just…" Her eyes clouded with sadness and she focused on the last sip of wine swirling in the bottom of her glass.

"You fell out of love with him?" Elle supplied.

"No, not exactly."

"You're still in love with him?"

"No, not that either." Ashley refilled her glass and drew out the silence. Elle took the chance to top off her glass as well. This woman was one surprise after the next, and she was betting her patience would pay off. "My love for David just wasn't that kind of love. We're wonderful friends. We grew up together. We were so young when we married. Too young. I thought that was what I was supposed to do. But as time went on we realized the truth—even though we cared deeply about each other, what we shared wasn't romantic love. After that it was just me slowly dying inside. I wasn't meant to spend my life like that with David. Or any man. As you probably know, I'm a lesbian."

Elle was touched by Ashley's honesty. The way she was willing to open up and be raw and true in front of her was brave. And admirable. Maybe foolish, but Elle wasn't judging. She appreciated it when people were honest with her. She recalled hearing about the reality television couple divorcing and Ashley coming out. She seemed to remember the show had a brief spike in popularity after that, but apparently it didn't last. "Do you think it's the lesbian part that's scared your viewers off?"

Ashley's ruby red lips puckered temporarily before she answered. Her mouth looked really fucking kissable like that. "Jill says it's not the lesbian thing so much as the divorce thing. The audience seemed to take my coming out just fine. And as long as people were watching, the network didn't really care what I did. But I guess when it came down to it, the audience only liked David and I as a set, living the fantasy of a perfect couple with a perfect home." She gave a wry smile. "At least the audience took my coming out a lot better than my parents did. My father basically pretends to this day that I didn't come out to him. My mom tut-tutted when I first told them I was a lesbian and said I'd regret airing my personal business all over town. I reminded her that I was on a reality TV show, so my business was already out there anyhow. These days she just ignores it as best she can. Changes the subject when she can't."

Elle dipped her head to catch Ashley's watery gaze. Their fingers grazed on the couch cushion between them and Elle's heart skipped a beat. Taking Ashley's hand in hers felt right. "I'm sorry about the way your parents reacted. That's got to hurt."

Ashley gave a half-hearted shrug. "Jill says I should give them time to sit with it. Maybe they'll come around."

"But, getting back to the future of your show, you told me what Jill thinks, but what do you think?"

That beautiful mouth pressed into a sad smile and she blinked several times. Not foolish. Definitely brave. "I think the show has run its course, but that doesn't mean I'm ready to let it go." She shifted on the couch, tucking one foot beneath her. Casual and real. And close. Her knee bumped against Elle's thigh and sent a jolt of pleasure straight to her core. "*Queen of the Castle* is the last piece of my old life still standing, and even though I'm excited for whatever comes next, the show is like a security blanket. It feels comfortable and safe. It's hard to let go. I'm not ready."

"Yeah, I get that." Elle nodded. "Change is hard. For viewers and for us."

Queen of the Castle was Ashley's safety net and she was afraid to make the jump without it. Elle could understand that, especially since losing the gig on the *Dog Tails* reboot felt like her own safety net had been yanked out from under her. But Ashley didn't seem like the kind of woman who needed a safety net. She would find her next step, no problem. She just needed to realize that for herself. After all, she was handy and resourceful, and…gorgeous. Elle's fingers brushed Ashley's thigh in what she meant to be a comforting touch, but it was like electricity zapped through her when they connected. It stirred something in her and she leaned in closer, suddenly wanting more.

"It *is* hard. Even when you're…" Ashley's tongue darted out and moistened her lips as she closed the gap between them. "Excited."

Elle's pussy clenched and she closed her eyes, ready to make contact with that alluring mouth. But before the fantasy became reality, the kitchen timer buzzed making them both jump and shattering the moment. Elle's brain sputtered as it came back to the present. Back to clarity. She said the first thing that popped into her head, "I guess it's time to sauté the pearl onions and mushrooms."

"What?" Ashley was blinking again, apparently having trouble recovering as well.

"The boeuf bourguignon." Elle hopped up from the couch. Back to business. What had she been thinking anyway? She had to stop entertaining these thoughts about Ashley. They were coworkers for fuck's sake. Business and pleasure did not mix. At least it sure never led to anything good. "We better get back to it."

Elle had stayed and helped Ashley clean up her kitchen after dinner, but that was it. With a weak excuse about wanting to be there when Luci got back from the movies, she headed home. But returning home early meant Elle ended up sitting alone in her kitchen, her mind swirling with thoughts of the day.

She'd had a good time cooking with Ashley, and once they got past that almost kiss on the couch they'd gone right back to easy conversation over dinner. Elle had held up her end of the bargain and taught Ashley how to make a delicious dish for Stew Week on *Celebrity Cook Off*. So why did she feel like there was something she was forgetting to do? Like there was a piece of the puzzle still missing. She was wondering if it had something to do with not following through with insisting Ashley order some new shoes, when Luci came in through the side door.

"Mom," she said tossing her backpack onto the sideboard. She climbed onto one of the stools at the kitchen island. "Are you seriously waiting up for me?"

"You're barely sixteen years old and out on a date. I'm your mom. Of course I'm waiting up for you."

"It's not even late and besides, it wasn't a date. It was just a hang. I mean, it was Benji."

"Mmhmm. I agree it's not late, but I'm not buying the not-a-date thing. I don't know what exactly a 'hang' is, but I see the way you look at that kid. And the way he looks at you." Elle leaned against the counter and crossed her arms. She remembered all too well what it was like to be a teenager with a crush and raging hormones. "So you best believe I'm keeping an eye on the situation."

Luci rolled her eyes. "Mom. That's so unfair. Did Grandma do that to you when you were sixteen?"

"Not exactly. When I was sixteen I was pregnant with you." Elle watched her daughter's mouth open and close wordlessly. She had rendered her teenager speechless. Total rare event. Luci knew the story, of course, but perspective could be a hell of a thing. She let Luci sit with the feeling for a beat before pushing off the counter and kissing the top of her head. "But just because it worked out wonderfully for me doesn't mean that it's the right path for everyone."

"Mom! It wasn't even a date!"

"Want some ice cream?" Elle ignored her daughter's protest and scooted across the kitchen and peered in the freezer for the carton. "All we have is vanilla though."

Luci slid off her stool and headed for the pantry. "Please. You've taught me better than that. You get the big bowl. I'll get the chocolate chips and peanut butter."

"Oh, grab the pretzels too."

They worked together combining the ingredients, folding them all into the ice cream and in no time they had a decadent treat.

Luci handed her mom a spoon and settled back on her seat at the island. "So how was your dinner?"

Elle licked peanut butter from her spoon. "The dinner part of the evening went well."

"The dinner part?" Luci's eyebrows shot up with interest. The kid was too clever for her own good. "What other part was there?"

"Well, there was some…awkward conversation." Elle sighed when her daughter continued to stare and wait for her to say more. "Ashley's show might get canceled, so she's on the edge of a big change in her life. You know, I can totally understand how she feels. Starting over is scary, but she'll be fine. She's smart and can do amazing handy things around the house. And she's fun to hang out with."

"Oh my God, you like her!"

Elle choked on her ice cream. "What?"

"I wondered when you put on mascara to go to your friend's house and cook. You never wear mascara when you go to Aunt Mari's. But now that you're talking about Ashley, your face looks the same way I feel about Benji. You *like* her."

She *liked* Ashley Castle? It explained why she couldn't stop thinking about what it might have been like to kiss her alluring mouth. But *like* her? Was that why she felt like she wanted to do more for her than just teach her how to make a fancy French stew? Not in a dirty way. Well, a little in a dirty way. What she really wanted was to help Ashley do whatever would help her transition from *Queen of the Castle* to whatever was next for her. If that meant continuing on in the cooking competition, then Elle wanted to help her do that. They would just have to figure out how to fit in more cooking classes between filming. Because they were coworkers. Coworkers. There was the buzzkill. She knew better than to get involved with someone with whom she was working. It had bitten her in the ass before. Elle needed the television exposure from being on *Cook Off* as much as Ashley did. She didn't want to do anything to mess that up for either of them. But apparently she…liked Ashley. And now she was going to have to figure out a way to deal with that.

"Mom. Admit it. You like Ashley."

"I would admit it, but then you'll have to admit you like Benji." She smirked. "I just don't want to do that to you."

"That's very generous of you," Luci quipped. Like mother, like daughter. Elle couldn't be prouder. Luci pushed her empty dish aside and pointed her spoon toward her mother's bowl. "Can I have some of your ice cream?"

Elle laughed and pulled her dessert out of her daughter's reach. "Oh, honey, I'm not THAT generous."

CHAPTER TEN

Ashley had meant to make her call time at the studio Monday morning. She really did. She was up and dressed, had a healthy breakfast of yogurt and a banana, and was heading out the door when her phone rang. It was David.

"How's everything going there?" His voice was gentle. He knew she was sitting around fretting about *Queen of the Castle*. She could hear it in his voice.

"You know."

"I know," he confirmed. "You're going to totally stress yourself out. There's nothing we can do about it now but wait, so please try to relax a little. And listen, Ash, I will do whatever you want, but think about what I said. Maybe it's time to let it go. I heard from my agent this morning and I've got a couple offers out there. If I accept any of them I'm going to be really thin for time on *Queen of the Castle*. There are other things we could do, and it's okay to move on. Hallmark is always chasing you down for movies. Or you could do whatever else you want. I just want you to be happy, and hanging on to the past might not be the best course for that."

Ashley smiled against the phone. He really was a good friend—supportive and truthful, even when the truth was tough. "I want you to be happy too, David. You do whatever you need to with the offers you're getting. It's okay—we'll figure this out. I'm not ready to give up yet. I've still got a trick or two up my sleeve."

"I'm sure you do." His low laugh drifted across the line. "What have you gotten yourself into this time?"

"I'm on a cooking competition show on the Eats! Channel."

"Cooking competition?" David didn't even try to hide his guffaw. "You can't even cook spaghetti hoops."

"You know what they say, 'fake it 'til you make it.'" Ashley tried to sound light and breezy. It wasn't much of a plan, but it was the best she had.

"If anyone can do it, you can." There was a reason he'd been her best friend all these years. David remained her rock. "Keep me posted."

The minute she hung up she drove to the studio and rushed to the makeup trailer as fast has her brand-new spiral art Tretorn Nylites would carry her. Thanks to Elle's advice and a little time Insta-stalking Reese Witherspoon, she'd bought the sneakers on Sunday afternoon. They were paying off already, ferrying her comfortably and quickly onto the set.

Fresh-faced and ready to go, she glanced down at her colorful shoes and pushed through the doors to the *Cook Off* set. She couldn't stop the smile tickling at the corners of her mouth. It was definitely Elle's influence that had led her to expand her style choices and…she liked that. Heat flushed her cheeks. What was it about that woman that made Ashley want to follow her every command? It was one of her favorite things about being in the kitchen with Elle. That confident way Elle had of issuing orders in her sexy low register—it made more than one part of Ashley take notice.

After Ashley aproned up at her workstation, she took a deep breath to calm her racing heartbeat and surveyed the space around her. With the exception of young Benji, all competitors were accounted for. Freddie Simon was nowhere in sight, but that wasn't unusual. He made a habit of popping in just before the cameras started rolling. Too cool to hang out with the others unless absolutely necessary. From day one Freddie had made it clear he felt he was the brightest star in the *Celebrity Cook Off* universe. For as vibrant and warm a host he appeared to be on television, his real-life personality left more than a little to be desired.

"I was starting to think you weren't going to join us today." Elle casually drifted over to Ashley's station.

"Doesn't look like I missed much. What's going on?"

"Not sure." Elle shrugged. "Waiting on you and Benji, I guess. No one from production has actually said anything about getting started. But I'm glad we have a minute to talk. I had an idea I wanted to run past you."

An idea? After the way Elle had made a mad dash out of her house Saturday night Ashley hadn't expected to be recruited by her as a coconspirator anytime soon, but here they were. "Is everything okay?"

"Everything's totally okay. I just feel bad that I only showed you how to make one dish. Now that I know why you need to stay in the competition so badly I want to do something more to help. You know, since you're on a cooking competition but you don't know how to—"

"Hey!" Ashley reached across the counter separating them. Maybe she could grab that last word right out of her mouth. "Keep it down. It's called a deep dark secret for a reason."

Elle made a motion with her hand like she was zipping her lips shut and throwing away the key. She leaned in and lowered her voice. "Okay, okay. Here's the thing: we both need to stay on the show as long as possible to reap the benefit of exposure. So it seems like we are in direct competition. But only three of us here are going to make it to the last episode. There's no reason two of those people can't be you and me. After that, it maybe doesn't matter who wins."

Making it to the show's finale seemed like the longest of long shots, but it also caused Ashley's heart to skip with excitement. An alliance with Elle held some appeal—she liked the thought of conspiring with her. If only there wasn't that one giant roadblock standing in the way of her making it to the last episode. "There is one reason." She hushed her voice down to a sharp whisper, "I can't cook."

"I believe we've covered that," Elle deadpanned. "The thing about cooking is, if you have a few solid dishes in your repertoire and know a handful of basic tricks, you should be able to adapt to any curveballs the competition throws us. I can teach you those things. We'll have a hell of a week squeezing in cooking lessons between our Monday and Wednesday shooting schedule this week, but we can make it work."

Even Elle's plan sounded like a recipe. A cup of solid dishes, a tablespoon of tricks, a pinch of dumb luck. But anything was better than Ashley's current plan which was basically "Get through the stew episode and hope for the best after that." If Elle was willing to volunteer her free time to help, she would take it. Ashley mentally added Elle's winning qualities to her recipe for success: a dash of cool confidence, a sprinkle of sexy smiles. It just might work.

"Earth to Ashley." Elle waved her hand in front of her face. "What do you think? Are you in?"

Did she really have any choice? She didn't have anything else to do with that "free time" anyway except sit around and worry about the fate of her show. David had been right that morning—she was becoming more and more stressed out about something that was out of control at this point. The busier she was, the better. There was just one part that was giving her pause. "Why are you doing this? Why are you being so nice to me?"

Elle's excited expression dropped as if she didn't exactly know the answer to that either. Slowly, her shoulders crept up to an unsure shrug. "You were nice to my kid and you weren't completely unbearable to hang out with last weekend." She cracked a teasing smile. "I guess I just want to help because... we're friends."

Elle was actually saying they were friends? That was different. Sure, Ashley had used the word to describe them, but up to this point it had always been met by a stubborn eyeroll from Elle. Was this the same woman who only four days earlier said there was "nothing between them" and nearly slammed the door in her face? She didn't know what was behind Elle's change of heart, but she was more than willing to roll with it. "Then I guess I'm in."

"Great. We can start tomorrow and—"

"Can I have everyone's attention please?" Producer Kelly stood at the front of the set with her hands clapped around her mouth to amplify her voice. "I just need a minute and you can be on your way. I'm sorry to announce that Benji Daniels has been taken to the hospital with suspected poisoning and will be unable to film today. As such, we're going to shut down until we have him back with us."

The competitors' incredulous murmurs buzzed through the set, but former boy-band member Mason Getty spoke up loud and clear. "Come on. We already showed up for the shoot today, can't we just do our thing and you guys can edit him in or whatever later?"

"God, Mason." Elle shot eye daggers across the aisle. "Real nice. He's a kid for God's sake."

"Settle down, guys," Kelly continued. "We're unsure when he'll be back or even if he'll be able to come back, but for now we're in wait-and-see mode. Benji brings in the young viewers and that's a demographic we need to grab. We don't want to do this without him."

"Holy shit!" Elle mouthed over her shoulder. "*If?*"

Ashley hadn't missed that part either.

"Go home. We'll call you when we have an update."

Elle turned to Ashley as she pulled her apron off. Her eyes were full of concern. "Poor kid. I hope he's okay."

"I know. Poisoned? Like someone poisoned him?" Ashley shook her head in disbelief. Why would anyone do that to a teenager? Fear shivered down her spine. Did this have something to do with *Celebrity Cook Off*? Were they all in danger? She tried to recall if she'd seen the security guard who normally worked the entrance when she entered the studio that morning. She'd been in such a rush it was all a blur. "What the hell?"

"Hey." Elle reached across the countertop and grabbed her hand. The touch was immediately calming. "She didn't say someone poisoned him. She said 'suspected,' so maybe that's not it at all. Maybe it's just a bad case of the flu."

"Okay. That's possible. But 'suspected' sounds a lot like there's a 'suspect' and that would mean someone poisoned him."

"Panicking isn't going to help anything." Elle pulled her phone out of her back pocket and checked the time. "And speaking of panic, I've got about five hours before Luci gets home and I have to tell her about Benji. Looks like we've been gifted some time, and I know I could use a distraction. Let's go to my house and get cooking."

Ashley set a steaming mug of coffee on the counter in front of Elle and stirred sugar into her own. Thanks to Elle's supply of frozen homemade pie dough, they were well on their way to making quiche in the Bissett kitchen. Since Ashley had learned to make pie crust from Chef Sarah, she didn't feel she was missing out on instruction in that area. Instead, Elle wanted to help her with what she called "go-to moves" in the kitchen.

Elle had just finished rolling the pie dough out and filling it into the pie dish. "Okay. I'm going to stick this in the fridge to chill, then we're going to make the best caramelized onions in the world with the help of everyone's best friend, bacon."

While Elle had her head in the fridge, Ashley eyed up the smattering of photos stuck to its door with tourist magnets. Most of the pictures were Luci, but Elle was in a handful of them as well. Mother and daughter grinning at the camera at a park, in the stands of a baseball game, dressed up at an event at Luci's school. It was clear that Elle and her daughter spent a lot of time together and shared a special bond.

"The key to making crispy, sizzling bacon in a cast-iron skillet is to bring them up to temperature together," Elle continued as she breezed around the kitchen and grabbed what she needed. "Starting at a low temperature releases the fat. The bacon cooks in its own fat. It's a beautiful thing. Poetic, really. Once it really gets going we'll increase the heat to crisp it up."

"I've never cooked in a cast-iron skillet," Ashley confessed. She admired how Elle operated so smoothly and confidently in the kitchen. Like she'd been doing it her whole life. She appreciated that Elle was willing to give her whatever stolen moments they could find in their shooting schedule, but would they really add up to enough to keep her in the competition? It seemed iffy at best.

"I love my cast iron. It belonged to my mother. She used it for everything, and I do too."

While Elle finished the bacon, Ashley chopped the asparagus for the quiche. She knew enough to start by cutting off the woody ends, but after that she was just guessing. Chopping was chopping, right? Was that even the right term when it came to asparagus? "Cutting" seemed pedestrian. "Slicing" didn't sound right either. "Chopping" had to be it. But based on the way Elle was eyeing her up something about her technique wasn't quite on point. "What? I know you want to say something so have at it."

Elle pulled the last of the bacon from the pan, carefully placing it on a plate covered with paper towels to rest before sidling up to the kitchen island. "I don't want to *say something*. I want to teach you proper knife handling. That's what you're here for, right?"

There was starting to be many reasons for Ashley to be there in Elle's kitchen. Of course, there was the fact that she needed all the help she could get as far as cooking went. But there was also the warm, cozy feeling anytime she ended up there—the wonderful smells, the delicious food, the easy vibe that made it feel like everyone was family in the Bissett home. Then there was the other thing, the most surprising part of all: she *liked* hanging out with Elle. That uneasy sense that they were still rivals from their teenage years had all but dissolved like sugar in boiling water. They were on an equal footing now. Well, except for the fact that Elle was an excellent cook and Ashley, not so much. So, yes, that was why she was there in Elle's kitchen. "Fair enough."

"Okay, grab an onion out of that bowl. I'm gonna help you with your form." She stepped behind Ashley and pressed close, wrapping her arms around to top Ashley's hands with her own. "Is this okay?"

Their hips bumped and pleasure bloomed in Ashley's core. It was very okay. She was also very glad she wasn't facing Elle so she wouldn't see the heat burning in her cheeks. "It's per…fine. It's totally fine."

Elle's laugh came out in a warm poof that played against Ashley's neck. She gripped the knife tighter to ground her focus.

"Fine? Okay. I'm just going to guide your hands." Elle's grip tightened as well. "I'm not going to hurt you. Promise."

Together they sliced the onion, root to tip in smooth, easy pulls. Ashley tried to keep her attention on the task at hand, but she was much more intrigued by how calm she felt enveloped by Elle's body. It wasn't awkward at all, more like another comfortable extension of being in the Bissett kitchen. Warm and welcoming. Natural.

"Grab two more," Elle instructed. "We'll only need a portion of them for the quiche, but you need the practice and I'll freeze the rest. You never know when you'll wish you had some caramelized onions tucked away in the freezer."

Ashley had never wished she had caramelized onions tucked away in her freezer, but she didn't say that out loud. Instead, she did as she was told, and tried to ignore how much she liked it when she stretched her spine and Elle's breasts pressed into her back.

They finished the task in silence. When the last cut had been made, Elle lingered behind her for a moment longer than necessary. Ashley didn't complain. Elle's soapy scent wrestled with the lingering onion aroma. The warm contact from being pressed together felt good as hell.

"Now for the magic," Elle whispered, building suspense as if she was about to divulge the most secret of family recipes. "We sauté the onion in the bacon grease. It takes them to the next level."

Ashley hated that their bodies separated, but the incredibly sweet smell of the onions cooking was a slight consolation. The rest of the quiche-making process went without a hitch and soon they were sliding the pie dish into the oven.

"And now we wait." Elle set the timer for thirty-five minutes and turned to face Ashley. As she looked her over, one side of her mouth immediately slid up into a smirk.

"I impressed you with my whisking skills, right?" Ashley couldn't take her eyes off those lips. They were full and had a natural rose hue with the perfect amount of gloss. Simply gorgeous and infinitely tempting.

"You have egg on your face."

"Okay, I admit my technique may not be perfect, but I got the job done. Certainly nothing I should be embarrassed about."

"I was impressed by your whisking skills, but…" Elle stepped closer and brushed her thumb across Ashley's cheek. "You have actual egg on your face."

Ashley held her breath as Elle's hand slid from her cheek to behind her head and tangled in her hair. Their gazes locked and Elle bit her bottom lip. The very thing she had longed for as a teenager—a kiss from her first crush, Elle Bissett—was about to happen. Her chest tingled like the bubbles in a glass of champagne as she leaned in ready for the delicious contact. She could feel the warmth of Elle's breath on her lips and—

"Mom!"

The women jumped apart as Luci crossed the kitchen in three strides.

Elle seemed to find her voice first. "Why aren't you at the beach? I thought you were going to be gone all day."

"Mom, Benji's in the hospital!" Her eyes filled with tears. She looked so fragile and scared. "He's really sick. Everybody's posting about it online."

"Oh, honey." Elle took her daughter in her arms and hugged her tight. Over Luci's shoulder she shot Ashley a distressed grimace that seemed to apologize for the interruption. It was unnecessary. Her daughter needed her. Ashley understood that. "They told us at work that he was in the hospital. I should've let you know."

"We have to go see him."

"We will," Elle said into the top of her daughter's head where she'd planted a kiss. "But we can't go right now. The doctors are taking care of him, don't worry. Until they figure out what's going on they're not going to let us see him anyway."

Ashley had to try something to comfort Luci. She pulled up her email on her phone. Luckily she found a little hope in her inbox. "Salmonella."

"What?" mother and daughter asked at the same time.

"I have an email from Kelly." Ashley scrolled and scanned to relay the scoop. "Benji has salmonella. He can't come back to *Cook Off* until he's symptom-free, so they're canceling production for the week. But the important thing is, Benji's going to be okay."

It was clear from Luci's furrowed brow she wasn't convinced. "What's salmonella?"

"It's a bacterial infection. Food poisoning. Knowing that kid he probably ate something he shouldn't have. Maybe undercooked chicken. Perhaps even raw, God knows…" Elle shook her head, but her expression was full of relief. "Listen, there's a bacon and asparagus quiche in the oven as we speak. Let's have some lunch and then you can text Benji and see how he's feeling."

Luci reluctantly agreed and slouched moodily against the kitchen island. While Elle set the table, Ashley poured three goblets of water.

Not having *Cook Off* film for a week was both a blessing and a curse. It gave Ashley more time to work on her culinary skills, but it also gave her a hell of a lot of free time to sit around and worry about her show.

"Hey." Elle had scooted up behind her when Luci left the kitchen to grab her phone. Her voice was low, careful to not be overheard. "I feel bad for Benji and his food poisoning, but this gives us exactly what we need."

"What we need?" Ashley repeated dumbly, the meaning of Elle's words lost on her. A need like what stirred in her when they had almost kissed? She needed that. Hell, she still couldn't shake the thought of it. That familiar pull in her chest kicked up once more now that Elle was near her again. But they couldn't exactly start making out when any minute Luci was going to join them for lunch.

"Yep." Elle nodded. "It gives us time for those cooking lessons we talked about. It's gonna be like kitchen boot camp. Just me and you, all week long."

Something about the way Elle's eyes seemed to go a shade darker when that sexy smirk spread across her face made a jolt of excitement shoot through Ashley's middle. More time alone with Elle? Yes. That was something she needed. But… "I can't ask you to give up your free time like that."

"You're not asking. I'm offering." Elle shrugged and her shoulder brushed against Ashley's back. Warmth spread through Ashley. What was the saying about standing the heat in the kitchen? "My current project is on hold and Lucy will be off surfing every day. You don't have a corner on the market for needing a distraction. I'm going to be here in my kitchen cooking all week one way or another. You may as well join me."

Ashley turned to face Elle to see if maybe it was all a joke, if those beautiful brown eyes were laughing at her, but that wasn't the case. All she saw was kindness. She couldn't deny she needed all the help she could get, and here the opportunity had been dropped in her lap. Who was she to question fate? "Kitchen boot camp? Sign me up."

A bright smile spread across Elle's face. "Great. We'll talk menu over lunch." She winked before turning her attention back to serving the quiche and excitement tickled at Ashley's spine again.

There was no doubt cooking lessons with Elle would be a *very* welcome distraction.

CHAPTER ELEVEN

"Tell me again what Benji was trying to do—The Rocky Challenge? What is that?" Ashley picked through the baskets of tomatoes, amazed by the variety offered at the booth. Every stand at the farmers' market Elle brought her to had been full of impressive produce, baked goods, and even treats like kettle corn or wine. There was a new delight every time she turned around. The goal of the excursion was to select ingredients for their next cooking lesson, but Ashley had quickly decided that the experience felt more like fun than an errand.

"The Rocky Challenge. The Laundry Pod Challenge, The Cinnamon Challenge. The kids just love a good Challenge these days. Why can't it ever be the Clean Room Challenge or the Good Grades Challenge?" Elle rolled her eyes and sniffed a bundle of mint. Her voice slid into that raspy register it always did when her dry humor came out. It made Ashley smile. "Apparently for this one you have to drink six raw eggs like Rocky Balboa did when he was training. Most kids probably can't even get six eggs down, much less keep them down. But you know Benji—he can eat anything. And because of that he got salmonella."

"So, technically he didn't keep them down permanently. Only Benji." Ashley selected one basket of heirloom tomatoes and one of cherry tomatoes after debating among the variety. The vibrant colors made her want to try them all. "Poor kid. That can be some nasty stuff. How's he doing?"

"We video chatted with him this morning." Elle added a bunch of carrots to her bag. Ashley was used to carrots in plastic bags that came from grocery delivery. These had the leafy green tops still on, like the kind you would see Bugs Bunny nibbling. "He still looked pretty green around the gills, but he was feeling good enough to brag about how many times he puked."

"I bet Luci was super impressed."

"I'm ashamed to say that child hung on his every word. Even the puking stories. She'd follow Benji to the far ends of the Earth." Elle shot Ashley a wry smile. "Don't worry, the minute we got off the call I hid our eggs before she could get any ideas about jumping on the Challenge bandwagon. Better safe than sorry."

A sign for fresh corn caught Ashley's eye. "Oh, do you like corn on the cob?"

"I like corn fresh off the cob." Elle nodded. "Why don't you grab some? We'll roast it and cut it off the cob to add to our salad tonight. An element like that can really take something like a boring salad to the next level."

"Sounds delicious," Ashley agreed. She grabbed a couple of ears and they carried their selection to pay the booth attendant.

"Elle! What brings you to the market on a Tuesday?" The old man in denim coveralls and a green cap was small in stature but had a big smile that made his eyes crinkle at the edges.

"Gus, my friend, how the heck are you?" Elle hauled her bag up onto the table to tally its contents.

"I'm good, so good." He nodded at Ashley. "And who is this young lady?"

"Oh!" Elle looped her arm through Ashley's and pulled her in. "Gus, let me introduce you to Ashley Castle."

"It's a pleasure, young lady. Such a pleasure." Gus took Ashley's hand in both of his. His touch was warm and strong, and she liked him immediately.

"The pleasure is mine." Ashley smiled back at him. He had an old-fashioned charm that she found delightful. "Your tomato selection is amazing and each one more beautiful than the next. I had a hard time deciding among them."

"Thank you, dear."

"Blakeslee Farms has been Gus's family business going on four generations," Elle explained. "His father entrusted it to him, and now his daughter is running it. And his grandson is studying agricultural business at the University of California. How is Trey? Is he done for the semester?"

"He got home last week and he's already giving his mother a run for her money." The more Gus spoke about his grandson, the more his eyes twinkled with joy. It was clear he was proud of his family. "He's got his head full of grand ideas like an online market. A farmers' market on the computer. Can you imagine? He says he's driving Blakeslee Farms into the future. He's driving his mother to want an early retirement if you ask me."

"She knows a thing or two about running a successful business." Elle laughed. "She'll rein him in."

It struck Ashley how good Elle was with people. She'd made fast friends with Benji day one on set and now he was practically family. It was much the same easy vibe she'd had with the folks at the farmers' market. It was quickly becoming one of Ashley's favorite things about her.

Gus tallied up their items and Elle paid the bill, but he didn't let them walk away without one last treat. "I almost forgot!" He exclaimed as he dug around under the table for something. "Remember the last time you were here and we got to talking about your chili recipe? I have some of my pickled hot peppers for you. Dice some of these up and sprinkle them on your bowl of chili before serving. That will dial the heat up right nice."

The bright gold, green, and red tones of the peppers made Ashley's mouth water. She hoped Elle would find a way to incorporate them into the pasta primavera they planned for dinner.

Elle took the jar in one hand and clapped the other on Gus's shoulder. "Thanks, friend. What would I do without you to spice up my life?"

Gus laughed a low, rumbly laugh and pointed back at her. "I see what you did there. I see. You ladies have a good afternoon now."

As they left the Blakeslee Farm booth, Elle's phone dinged with an alert. She poked at the screen and her face scrunched up in annoyance before she finally shook her head and gave whatever she was looking at an angry swipe before returning the phone to her back pocket.

"Everything okay?" Ashley couldn't bite back her curiosity. She hoped it wasn't something that would derail the plans they'd made for their day together. To her surprise, she was really looking forward to the cooking lessons.

Elle chewed her bottom lip as if she was deciding whether or not to share, but then she sighed. "The Petersons keep emailing me about wanting to meet Luci."

"The Petersons, like, Josh Peterson's parents?"

"Yeah, Luci's grandparents. Technically speaking, of course. She doesn't know them at all. I've been ignoring them because I just don't know what to say. They haven't contacted me or shown any interest in her for all these years, and now all of the sudden they want to get together. It just feels weird to me, like something's off." Elle's sad eyes suggested there was a story there, but Ashley didn't want to overstep. If she wanted to tell it, she would.

"Maybe they're just wondering about her, or they want to see how you're doing?"

"Maybe. I'm not going to worry about it right now." Elle shook her head again like she was dismissing the topic. Her expression relaxed into a smile as she linked their arms. Ashley was starting to really enjoy their casual touching. "We have farm-fresh ingredients and a delicious dinner to make."

"Ready to head home then?" she asked.

"Just a quick stop for wine on our way out." Elle steered her toward their next destination. "It will be a reward for a job well done."

Back at Ashley's house, the women set to work preparing their farmers' market haul for the pasta primavera. Ashley racked up plenty of practice chopping carrots, zucchini, squash, onions, and broccoli. By the time Elle showed her how to toss the pasta with the veggies, and she'd added the freshly shaved parmesan cheese, Ashley felt she had indeed earned the delicious sauvignon blanc they'd picked up at the market.

"Hold on. I almost forgot," Elle said as she halted their plating progress to dig her phone out of her bag. "If I don't post a picture of this on Instagram, I will never hear the end of it."

"Luci's really pushing you hard on this one, huh?" Once again, Ashley found herself admiring the mother-daughter bond.

"Oh, she is so on my case about it." Elle snapped a few pics then started typing. "Hashtag pasta primavera. Hashtag homemade. Hashtag Elle is cooking."

"Um. What about, 'Hashtag Ashley cooked too'?" Ashley suggested with a teasing wink.

"My Insta, my hashtag." Elle stuck out her tongue and jabbed her finger at the phone again. "And post."

Ashley peered over Elle's shoulder as the picture zapped into the feed. "Wow, your food pics are amazing! Do you have a lot of followers?"

"Almost fifty thousand."

"After five days on the app you have *fifty thousand followers*? Impressive."

"*Almost* fifty thousand, I said." Elle shrugged. "The kids were right—people really like pictures of food. Speaking of good food, you did a great job with the veggies and we made a heck of a dish. Let's get it on the table. I'm starving."

Buzzing with pride in her cooking progress, Ashley had set the table for two using gold charger plates under their delicate china and crisp linen napkins. As a finishing touch, she lit the tall tapers in the candelabra in the center of the table. Romantic lighting? Maybe. She'd had a fun day with Elle, so why the hell not? Two friends could celebrate by sharing a nice meal without it being a big deal. Now as she carried the bread from the kitchen she hoped she hadn't overdone it.

Elle entered the dining room with a full plate for each of them and took her seat. As her gaze swept the table, her eyes sparkled. "Candles! So fancy." She raised her wineglass in Ashley's direction. "To a beautiful table, beautiful food, and my beautiful dining partner."

That was a lot of beautifuls. Ashley's chest went warm with more than just the effect of the wine. It was nice to have confirmation that the attraction she'd been feeling all day wasn't only one-sided.

"I'll drink to that. The dish looks delicious, and I feel like I'm really getting the hang of chopping and dicing. I might even be ready to...*julienne*." Ashley wiggled her eyebrows and was rewarded with Elle's throaty laugh. Another wave of heat washed over her.

"You're getting sassy." Elle saluted her with a forkful of pasta. A fitting response to culinary humor. "I like that."

Ashley twirled capellini on her fork and watched Elle's reaction to her bite. The way her lips pursed and her eyes rolled back in her head told her a story of pure bliss. "Tastes that good, huh?" She didn't wait for an answer. She tried the dish for herself.

Every over-enthusiastic word Elle had uttered earlier at the farmers' market about the superior taste of farm-fresh ingredients suddenly made perfect sense. The tomatoes were as juicy and sweet as they looked, and it turned out zucchini actually had flavor. Totally news to Ashley. But the real star of the show was Gus's pickled hot peppers. They added a slow heat that culminated in a real kick in the pants. The experience left her nearly speechless. "Whoa, the peppers!" She washed it down with a gulp of wine.

"Yeah, whoa." Elle nodded in agreement. "You can always count on Gus to come through with the flavor. But the veggies are absolutely superb. What did I tell you about vegetables straight from the farm?"

Ashley laughed and put her hands up in surrender. "I admit, you were right. I will never settle for sub-par produce again."

"Good girl," Elle said around a mouthful of pasta. "You've really come a long way from asking me about peppers for your chili that first day on set."

Heat crept up Ashley's neck and into her cheeks. She remembered that first day on set all too well: how she'd casually tried to strike up a conversation with Elle but instead ended up sounding like a total idiot. And then Elle suggested she was somehow trying to get her booted off *Cook Off.* Maybe not the greatest of memories. "Well, yes. I guess so."

"What's wrong? Why are you making that face and turning all red?" Elle's silverware clanked against her plate in alarm. "Are you choking?"

Ashley couldn't help but laugh at the way Elle was suddenly coiled up and ready to spring into action to save her. Elle had come a long way too. "I'm not choking. I was just remembering that day when I asked you about the peppers and the truth is—" Oh what the hell. She and Elle were different now than they were then. They were friends. Or something. "I was flirting with you."

"You were…flirting?" Surprise registered on Elle's face before it switched into a big, teasing grin. Half amused, half… flattered maybe? "That was you flirting with me?"

Elle was laughing at her, but it was better than reacting with a look of horror or running away screaming. Things could be worse. Still, Ashley wasn't quite ready to look Elle in the eye.

"Well, yeah. I guess I'm a little out of practice." She focused on spearing a piece of broccoli with her fork.

"Hey." Elle reached over and gave her forearm a quick but gentle squeeze. "I have faith you'll improve in that area too. And you're welcome to practice on me all you want."

A shock wave shot through Ashley from that point of contact on her arm, straight down between her legs. She had a sudden image of Elle clearing the dining room table with one sweep of her arm and topping her right there. She closed her eyes and took a good swallow of wine. The "practice flirting on me" comment was just more of Elle's teasing and twisted humor. It wasn't anything to get all worked up about. She had to change the subject, bring it back to something safer. Bring it back to the familiar. Elle moved her hand away and looked at her expectantly. Waiting for her to react. Ashley had been lost in her own thoughts and taken too long to respond. She was failing at flirting. Again. She had to say something. Anything.

"Cooking."

"What?" Elle's brows scrunched up in confusion.

"Um. I uh…" Crap. Get it together. She tried her awkward attempt to steer the conversation away from her awkward flirting again. "I was just thinking about all the different types of food I've cooked since we teamed up. Tex Mex, French, and now Italian."

"Actually, pasta primavera is a dish that was first served in New York City. Right here in the good ol' US of A." Elle paused to slurp a strand of pasta between her lips. Sexy, sexy lips. "I wouldn't have put an Italian meal on the table without serving cannoli for dessert." She sucked her bottom lip between her teeth and her eyes rolled in her head. It was like an…orgasm face.

"Cannoli? That's what does it for you?" Ashley laughed, relieved the spotlight was off her for the moment. "Cannoli?"

"Oh, yes!" Elle slapped both her palms on the table. She was clearly passionate about the dessert. "The first time I tasted cannoli, I thought I was in heaven."

"Your French mother made cannoli?"

"My French mother made a lot of things. She trained professionally as a chef before she moved here from France to marry my dad. But, no. I actually only had it for the first time about ten years ago in this wonderful little Italian restaurant in Westwood."

"In *Westwood*? I don't think I've ever eaten anywhere in Westwood."

"It's called Rocco's and everything they serve is so authentic, so rich and delicious. But the cannoli is…" Elle's face did the orgasm thing again and Ashley's belly fluttered. If the dessert was that good, it was definitely an *I'll have what she's having* situation. "You know what? I'm not gonna tell you about it, I'm gonna show you. I want to share this with you. Let's go to Rocco's."

"What, right now?" Ashley pulled her napkin from her lap and placed it neatly beside her plate. "We just ate, and you want to go to a restaurant? And what about Luci?"

"Luci is spending the night with her Aunt Mari to try to distract her from her Benji woes, so she's covered. And we're just going for dessert. Believe me, you won't regret it."

Ashley opened her mouth to protest on grounds of being underdressed for an evening out, but Elle had already pulled out her phone and was ordering them a rideshare. She had nothing holding her back, why not open herself to a little adventure and enjoy what Elle wanted to share with her.

"Our ride should be here in about eight minutes." Elle stood and began clearing the table.

"Perfect. Just enough time for me to run upstairs and change my outfit."

"Don't be ridiculous," Elle called over her shoulder as she headed to the sink.

"Come on." Ashley looked down with remorse at her faded jeans and purple Pumas. "At least my shoes."

"Absolutely not." Elle was by her side and grabbed Ashley's wrist before she could make a run for the steps. "The food at Rocco's might be to die for, but it's definitely a come-as-you-are kind of place."

Fancy clothes be damned. If the blast of excitement that shot through Ashley at Elle's touch was any indication of how the night was going to go, she was one hundred percent in, no matter what she was wearing. Hell, no clothes at all sounded fine by her if Elle was going to keep touching her. "Come as you are, huh?"

Elle's hand slid from Ashley's wrist to interlace their fingers. "You ready for it?"

Ashley wasn't sure if Elle was talking about the cannoli still, but either way she was sure of her answer. "I'm ready."

CHAPTER TWELVE

Elle leaned one elbow on Rocco's rustic mahogany bar and gazed at Ashley perched on the stool beside her and delicately sipping her wine. She never minded eating at the bar, but the way Ashley looked with the hazy glow of the hanging bulbs casting shadows around her made it even more appealing. Ashley was beautiful and sexy, and ever since she admitted she had been flirting with her that first day on set Elle couldn't stop thinking about taking her in her arms and kissing those full, ruby-red lips.

"What?" Ashley set her glass down. Her tongue darted out to capture a drop of wine left behind at the corner of her mouth. "Are you worried I'm going to finish my wine before the dessert comes?"

"Don't worry about that. There's plenty more where that came from." Elle took a sip from her own glass. She couldn't let a lady drink alone, plus the marsala was sweet and soothing like the arm of a friend slung easily around your shoulders. "Rocco will bring you whatever you want."

As if on cue, he appeared behind the bar and put their dessert between them. One plate and two forks. "That's right." His big smile softened the effect of his gruff voice and his strong arms strained the short sleeves of his white T-shirt as he leaned against the bar. He looked more like a bouncer than a cook, but he was magical in the kitchen. "Anything for my favorite customer." He gave Elle a wink. "How's that kid of yours, Elle?"

Luci was going to be mad when she found out she missed a trip to Rocco's, but that was future Luci. Current Luci was likely doing just fine under Marigold's good care. She swallowed her guilt and answered the question. "Well, she's with her Aunt Mari tonight, so she's probably living high on the hog. Do me a favor and don't tell her I came in here without her. There will be full-out hell to pay."

Rocco's gravelly laugh shook his big body. "She's with Mari? That kiddo's probably having the time of her life. But next time you bring her with you. I'll make her ricotta pie with pineapple—just the way she likes it. You two enjoy now."

As Rocco shuffled off, Elle caught Ashley staring at her with her lips lifted in a slight smile. It was Elle's turn to ask, "What?"

"Nothing." Ashley shrugged. "It's just everybody loves you. The farmers at the market, Rocco. You're obviously beloved."

"Eh. I like to eat and I get around." She was once again dazzled by the way the blue of Ashley's eyes were dotted with silver flecks. Like glitter. It was kind of…mesmerizing.

Ashley was the first to break eye contact. "All this dessert after everything else we've eaten tonight? Good thing we're sharing—I only expected one to be on the plate, not three."

"Well, if it was only one on the plate it would be cann*olo*. *Cannoli* is plural."

"No!" Ashley's lips formed a surprised "o" as if shocked by this grammatical revelation. "Cannolo?"

"Cannolo," Elle confirmed as her arm shot out to stop Ashley's hand reaching for her fork. "You're not going to need that. Rocco's cannoli are best enjoyed…organically."

Elle lifted one crispy shell and held it up in front of Ashley's lips. "Come on, give it a taste."

Ashley only hesitated a moment before leaning forward and taking a bite. Her eyes fluttered shut and she moaned with delight as she chewed. Creamy filling smeared on her upper lip and Elle brushed it away with a fingertip. Ashley licked her lips and moaned once more and the sound was like music to Elle's ears. Sexy music. She wanted to hear that sound again.

"See? I told you so," Elle said before taking her own bite. "Just like heaven."

"Totally." Ashley agreed. She grabbed Elle's wrist and pulled it back to her mouth for another taste. "The filling is so creamy, but the shell isn't soggy at all. It's such a beautiful contrast of textures."

"You're starting to sound like the *Cook Off* judges," Elle laughed. She'd noticed she'd been thinking in food-judge terms lately too, even when cooking or eating alone in her own kitchen. They'd both been brainwashed by their hours on the *Celebrity Cook Off* set. Maybe that also explained the intense attraction she was feeling to her coworker. Even as Ashley sat on a barstool with errant cannoli crumbs smudged on her mouth, she was as gorgeous as Elle had ever seen her. "But the reason they're so good is Rocco only fills the shells when you order. No chance to sit around getting soggy." She took another crispy bite to emphasize her point.

They went back and forth like that, taking turns enjoying bites until they'd devoured two of the cannoli. Elle licked some cream from her finger before pointing at the plate in a silent question.

Ashley held up a hand in protest. "I'm so stuffed, I couldn't possibly take another bite."

Elle hated to bring the night to a close, but they'd had a full day and dessert was clearly over. Plus, they could totally have the leftovers boxed up to take with them. "You ready to get outta here?"

"I guess so." Ashley nodded, but then seemed to reconsider. She looked up at her through her long lashes. "So Luci's not going to be home until morning?"

The smoldering look Ashley gave her stoked the flames of desire that had been building in Elle all night. "Mari's got her all night."

"Want to come back to my place?"

For the twenty-minute cab ride back to Bel Air, Elle and Ashley talked about the cannoli and other sweet treats they planned to make together, but Elle found that mostly she was trying really damn hard not to jump Ashley's bones right there in the back seat of the car. With each brush of their fingers on the seat and every time their knees bumped, the need inside her intensified. A familiar throbbing began between her legs, and she took a deep breath to steady her heartbeat. Even as the world zipped by outside, she couldn't take her eyes off Ashley's lips as she described her all-time favorite dessert, chocolate lava cake. The way she licked her bottom lip while talking about the gooey, fudgy center was enough to drive Elle completely wild. By the time they got to Ashley's house they tumbled through the door, barely able to keep their hands off each other.

"I have been waiting to do this all night," Elle said as she pulled Ashley to her. Her hands tangled in Ashley's long hair and at long last, she kissed her. Her tongue dipped between Ashley's full lips and she tasted the powdered sugar from the cannoli. It was sweet and hot, and so fucking worth the wait. She made quick work of unbuttoning Ashley's shirt as they continued to kiss and stumble toward the stairs.

Ashley moaned against her mouth as she shrugged out of her shirt, her breath sticky and sweet. "Why did we wait so long to do this?" she gasped as she led Elle to her bedroom.

"I don't know. We were very, very stupid."

Ashley's bedroom didn't look anything like it did on TV, at least not on the episodes Elle had seen. The floral prints were gone as were the piles of throw pillows. There was much less eyelet lace in general. The walls were now a bold lilac except for the portion surrounding the fireplace and the flatscreen TV mounted above it which was a vanilla cream white to match the trim. Ashley pushed at a panel on the wall as they entered. The crystal-tiered chandelier hanging in the center of the room came to life, providing the perfect romantic lighting. Elle had always thought chandeliers in any room other than a dining room or a grand foyer was a bit *extra*, but somehow in Ashley's bedroom it was a perfect fit. Classy, beautiful, and romantic—just like her.

"You've got way too many clothes on," Ashley said, tugging Elle's T-shirt over her head.

They stood facing each other in their jeans and bras. Elle saw her own desire reflected in Ashley's heavy-lidded blue eyes. Over Ashley's shoulder she caught a glimpse of them in the big, brushed-silver framed mirror propped in the corner of the room. Ashley's strong back with its defined muscles trailed down to a slim waistline. Back dimples peeked out above the low-slung denim. The indigo lace bra was a striking contrast against her creamy skin. For a moment Ashley's magnolia perfume seemed to beckon Elle, and from there it was on.

Elle grabbed Ashley's hips and pulled her against her. Their limbs tangled and the last of their clothes were tugged off and tossed aside. Lips met in a hungry kiss as they dropped onto the bed.

"You are so beautiful," she said, tucking a strand of hair behind Ashley's ear. Her gaze raked down her body, taking in every dip and curve. She nipped at Ashley's earlobe eliciting a sexy moan that made Elle's pussy clench. "I want you so badly."

"Then come get me," Ashley purred and pulled Elle on top of her.

Elle kissed her way down Ashley's neck while she pushed her knee between her thighs, surprised by how wet she was already. Clearly Ashley wanted her too. Excitement pulsed through her veins as her mouth found Ashley's breasts, teasing and licking on one nipple while massaging the other with her light fingertips. Ashley squirmed with anticipation beneath her. "Is this what you had in mind?" she gasped.

Ashley pulled Elle's hand to her lips and murmured against it, "Mmm, yes." She popped kisses on her wrist, then her elbow.

"And a little bit of this too." She pulled Elle up to lie beside her so they were face-to-face, and slowly trailed her fingertips down her chest to her abdomen.

Elle couldn't pinpoint the exact moment when her defensive wall had crumbled, but the constant tugging on her heart, the yearning to be in this woman's orbit was a certain sign that it had. It was like a force of nature. An earthquake tearing down that wall of old hostilities. It could just be that they hadn't really known each other back when they were teenagers. Ashley had shared how her life had changed since back then. She was a different woman now. Of course, there was the possibility Elle had changed too. They'd had different career experiences since being teenage television stars, but one thing was the same: they'd both grown up.

Elle's heart thumped as Ashley reached lower, inching closer to her heat. The anticipation was equal parts delicious and maddening. She couldn't wait any longer. She grabbed Ashley's ass and bumped their hips together, pressing Ashley's hand against her clit.

Not missing a beat, Ashley fluttered her fingers against her swollen, needy lips before mercifully pushing inside her. She kissed Elle again, this time thrusting her tongue into her mouth.

A wave of pleasure built in Elle, and she reached to find Ashley's wetness. She eased one finger into her. Then two.

They moved together, legs tangled up in the sheets, mouths obsessed with one another, each driving the other closer and closer to the edge. Finally, Elle gave in to the rush and cried out, squeezing Ashley's fingers as she orgasmed hard. Lights flashed behind her eyelids, and she struggled to keep the rhythm for Ashley who rode her hand a moment longer before reaching her own climax.

"Elle, yes!" She dug the fingers of her free hand into Elle's back as she tipped over the edge. The sound of her name in Ashley's breathless voice sent another quake of pleasure through Elle.

When they were both left panting, lying on their backs, and glowing with satisfaction, Elle found her words again. "I did not think this was going to happen."

Ashley giggled beside her. "Me neither. But I'm damn glad it did. Hell, a week ago I thought you couldn't stand me and now..."

Right. That's because then all she could think about when she looked at Ashley was how she took the role that was supposed to be hers. Before Elle's jealousy could stir up again, Ashley's hand slipped into hers. Their fingers intertwined as she gave her a squeeze. That bitter feeling that had started bubbling up in Elle's belly subsided replaced by something warm and... hopeful. Maybe it was finally time to let go of the past.

CHAPTER THIRTEEN

When Elle had first suggested the kitchen boot camp, Ashley thought the wording was largely hyperbole, but by day three of their cooking adventures she realized Elle was not fooling around.

Tuesday was a lesson in making a cake from scratch, including American buttercream frosting so white and fluffy it was like a sugary cloud on which you could float away. On Wednesday they'd tackled other desserts, starting with cannoli, of course, then moving on to standards—cupcakes, brownies and chocolate chip cookies. The pictures Elle posted on social media got thousands of likes and both women took pride in the praise of the comments.

Elle also made her practice, practice, practice those standard techniques until the kitchen table looked like they were hosting a bake sale. When Ashley worried that they'd made more than they could possibly ever consume, Elle assured her she had a plan that would make certain nothing went to waste.

Best of all, any concern Ashley might have had that there would be awkwardness between them after their intimate night evaporated the moment Elle had pulled her into her kitchen the morning after and greeted her with a warm, definitely more than just-friendly kiss. They'd worked side by side all day, same as usual, only with a few more teasing touches.

It had been the same thing Thursday morning. They'd met at the farmers' market to grab the eight pounds of fresh Roma tomatoes to make homemade spaghetti sauce. They'd even held hands as they walked through the market, until they had to let go to carry their haul. As they walked from one booth to the next, Ashley's heart was full of so much joy she wondered if she was literally glowing.

Back at home in her kitchen, Elle had slid back into drill-sergeant mode instructing Ashley to hone her basic knife skills by chopping onions and mincing garlic. Knife handling still didn't feel second nature to Ashley, but even she had to admit she'd improved since being under Elle's tutelage.

Actually, Elle had taught her a thing or two out of the kitchen as well. Ashley's body flushed warmly when she thought back three nights ago when Elle's magic hands had caressed and teased, worked her body to the brink and tipped her over it again and again. It was a feeling she hoped to revisit with Elle again soon.

"What is that look on your face? Is everything okay over here?" Elle had left her post at the stove and was now peering over Ashley's shoulder at her progress with the garlic. As Ashley's mind wandered her knife work had become a little… enthusiastic. "Yeah, that's minced. You can stop now."

Ashley set her knife down and inspected her final product. Embarrassed heat burned her cheeks. The garlic looked seconds away from being pulverized. She made a mental note to work on her ability to focus while she worked. "Great. What's the next step?"

"Have you ever peeled tomatoes? The water is almost boiling, and I've got the ice bath set up and ready to go. I'm going to show you how to blanch them to make them easier to peel."

The only Blanche that Ashley knew was the one on Golden Girls, but she kept that thought to herself and took the smaller knife Elle handed her. She wrinkled her nose at the little blade, turning it over in her palm. "Can't I just use the knife I used on the onions and garlic? We don't have to dirty another one."

Elle rolled her eyes and picked up her own knife. "Ash, the right tool makes the task easier, not to mention it gets the job done correctly. These are paring knives. We're going to dig the core out of one end of the tomato and score the other." She moved swiftly working the blade on the tomato, showing Ashley how it was to be done.

By the time they had worked through the entire eight pounds of tomatoes, the water was at a full rolling boil and Elle showed her how to drop batches of three into the pot for just a fraction of a minute before plunging them into the bowl of ice water. Ashley was surprised by how easily the skin peeled off.

"This is amazing. I thought it would take us forever to get through this pile," Ashley said, eyeing up the tomato in her hand. "But I'm not sure they look as beautiful naked like this."

"I agree, but removing the peel does wonders for the texture. You'll thank me when the sauce is done." Elle took a moment and seemed to study the skinless tomato. "Honestly, it does kind of remind me of that old gross-out Halloween party game where you peel grapes and people feel them and you say it's a bowl full of eyeballs."

"*Bowl full of eyeballs?*" Surely she had misheard. "What the heck kinda freaky-assed party games do you play?"

Elle laughed. "I said it was a Halloween party game. It's supposed to be disgusting. You know, you can't see what you're touching and you're told it's one thing like eyeballs, but it's really just peeled grapes. Or you're told it's witches fingers, but it's really just baby carrots. We used to play it every year for Luci's school class Halloween party. The kids loved it."

"You basically pranked innocent little schoolchildren by telling them they were touching something horrifying," she teased. "Well done."

"I'm telling you, they loved it. The game was a huge hit every single year." Elle's expression shifted and her eyes crinkled, obviously reflecting fondly on times gone by. "Then, of course, there would always be at least one kid in the class who would reach in at the end of the game and pop a handful of grapes in his mouth, bragging that he ate eyeballs. I can't believe you've never heard of the game."

Ashley shrugged. The prep school she'd attended did not host classroom parties. They were more of an all-business, no-nonsense type of educational institution. "I went to dull private schools all the way through. I guess Halloween games are something I missed out on."

Meanwhile, Elle was frowning. "Tell ya what. Next Halloween we'll throw a party here and you can be first in line to play the What Am I Touching game."

It was early June. Halloween was still several months away, and well after *Celebrity Cook Off* wrapped. But Elle was talking like it was a sure thing that they would still be hanging out together. Ashley couldn't stop the smile that split her face in two. "That sounds like a deal to me."

With Ashley's spirits restored, they moved on to the next step in the sauce-making process—squashing the peeled tomatoes into the pot with their bare hands. Ashley wasn't super excited about participating in the squishing, but she was flying so high from Elle making plans for the two of them several months into the future, she went along with it.

When their hands were covered in tomato juice and they had eight pounds of well-textured pulpy fruit in the pot, they mixed in the sauteed onions and garlic. Elle instructed Ashley to stir in sugar, and fresh oregano, thyme, and basil, explaining how each ingredient would enhance the flavor. Once again Ashley was impressed by Elle's knowledge and passion for cooking, and she had to admit, the more she learned and put the techniques into practice, the more natural it felt to her too.

"We're going to let this simmer for about three hours." Elle clapped a metal lid on top of the pot. "And while it does that, we'll make our spaghetti."

By the time the sauce was done simmering and the last batch of pasta was drying on the rack, Luci had returned from surfing at the beach. She dropped her bag by the door and draped her beach towel over one of the chairs at the kitchen table, barely saying hello as she marched straight to the fridge for a snack. Apparently, a day of surfing worked up a hearty appetite. She stopped raiding the fridge long enough to sniff the air. "Something in here smells amazing. What's for dinner?"

"We made sauce." Ashley grinned, proud to have another culinary accomplishment under her belt.

Luci emerged from the fridge with a ripe peach and scooted to the stove to lift the lid on the sauce pot. "Whoa. You made *a lot* of sauce. Are we expecting guests for dinner?"

"Nope. But we're definitely going to feed more people than just us," Elle answered cryptically. "Why don't you shower up, Lu? We could use some extra hands. Then when we get back home the three of us will have our dinner."

"When we get back home?" Ashley was intrigued. Elle hadn't steered her wrongly on an adventure yet.

The fifteen-minute ride in Ashley's SUV led them to a winding driveway, and as the vehicle approached the large residence the pieces fell into place for Ashley. "This is a women's shelter."

"Yep." Elle pointed to the path on the right to direct her around the Tudor-style building toward a service entrance in the back. "I called this morning and let the director know we'd be delivering a pasta meal."

"And a bakery," Luci said, patting the previous day's boxes of cookies and cupcakes on the leather seat next to her.

"Do you think maybe we overdid it?" Ashley steered along the gravel drive.

"Oh, please. This is nothing." Elle waved a dismissive hand in the direction of the back seat. "Right after Mom passed away, to get through the days, I baked like it was my job. I made trips over here with pies and cakes every other day."

"Baking sounds like a healthy way to deal with grief." Ashley nodded. Although Elle's tone had been matter-of-fact, she knew there was still a wealth of emotion bubbling just under her cool surface. Working through grief took time. "And I'm sure the results were much appreciated."

As if on cue a short, gray-haired woman waddled out of the back door, waving her hands enthusiastically.

Luci stuck her head out the window and called out, "Hey, Nan!"

"They do seem to know you here." Ashley pulled up to the edge of the cement walkway.

"Come on, I'll introduce you," Elle said as they all climbed out of the SUV.

"You brought a friend." The old woman's voice was about three octaves higher than what Ashley expected. "What a wonderful surprise."

"Good to see you, Nan." Elle wrapped her arms around the woman in a full-on bear hug. "I brought food and my friend Ashley."

When Elle released her, Nan reached out a hand to Ashley. "Truth be told, I recognized you the minute you pulled up," she said with a wink. "I'm a huge *Queen of the Castle* fan."

"That's very sweet," Ashley said but the handshake was interrupted when Luci squeezed between them to hug Nan. "It looks like you have some fans of your own."

"Oh, I've known this little lady since she was a wee one." Nan planted an affectionate kiss on the top of Luci's head. "Both of them, really."

"It's true." Elle nodded. "After my dad passed, Nan gave my mom a job here heading up the kitchen. It was perfect because we didn't have any family in the area to help take care of me, and Nan let my mom put me in the daycare here at the shelter free of charge. She worked here for years until my acting career started taking off and she had to stop this job to manage it. Then my mom started bringing me here again when I was pregnant with Luci. We baked a ton those nine months and God knows I was big enough without eating it all. It was a match made in heaven."

"Believe me, we always have plenty of hungry mouths to feed." Nan's laugh was like one of those jingling bells over a store door. It had a twinkling quality, what Ashley imagined a fairy would sound like laughing. "Come on, ladies. Let's get this food into the kitchen."

Elle and Nan chattered away as they carried dinner inside. Elle seemed just at home in that kitchen as in her own. She pulled trays out of a cabinet and carefully arranged their desserts on them. Once again Ashley marveled at how well Elle seemed to fit in everywhere they went. Elle's people skills were admirable and, judging by the way Luci was holding an animated conversation with Nan as they pulled out pots to warm the pasta and sauce, the apple hadn't fallen far from the tree. Ashley was filled with warmth, proud to be in the company of these generous, poised women. Sharing the results of their kitchen boot camp with the women's home was brilliant, and Ashley was so happy to be part of caring for others in a way she had never experienced.

A quick thirty minutes later they were heading back to Elle's with the satisfaction of sharing with others. Maybe they were all reflecting on that feeling in the silence which settled over them as they drove. When both Elle and Ashley's phones beeped at the same time it seemed to startle them all.

"That's a hell of a coincidence." Elle fumbled in her jacket pocket for her phone. "Group text from Kelly, 'Check email for production update.'" She paused to roll her eyes before she quipped, "How fun. It's like a digital scavenger hunt."

"What's the email say, Mom?" Luci inched forward on the back seat to look over her shoulder at the message.

Elle pressed her phone to her chest, hiding the screen. "Do you have your seat belt on?" She gestured at her daughter. "Sit back in your seat properly."

It seemed an unusually harsh response from the usually sanguine Elle. Luci's face squished, signaling her confusion, but she scooted back in her seat as she was told. After the click of the seat belt, Elle quickly read the message before summing it up for the other two.

"Oh, okay! Benji is officially cleared for return and we're back on set Monday morning. We're shooting Monday, Wednesday, Friday, and the finals will be filmed the following Monday."

"That's not so bad," Ashley said with a shrug while keeping her eyes on the road. She wished nothing but a quick recovery for Benji, but she had been hoping the producers would spread the filming out a bit to help fill her time. "That's only a few days over the original production schedule."

"And that gives us a whole weekend to prepare for the finale." Elle grinned. "Which is great because we are *doing this thing*. We are going all the way!"

From the back seat Luci let out a loud, "Whoop!" Then both Elle and Ashley joined in with the celebration. They were all still cheering and hooting when they pulled into Elle's driveway.

"I'm gonna go call Benji. I bet he's excited to get back in the studio!" Luci flew out of the car the second it came to a complete stop.

"Say hi from us," Elle called after her. She was waiting for Ashley to come around from the driver's side before heading to the house. "She's over us. We've been dumped for Benji."

"They're cute together," Ashley said, following her to the front door. Now that it was just the two of them, she could ask the question she'd been wanting to ask since Elle checked her email. "You held that phone screen against you like it held the Bissett family's secret chili recipe. What was in your email that you didn't want Luci to see?"

Elle groaned. "Another email from Janet Peterson. Same thing as before, she would like to meet Luci. Blah, blah, blah."

Ashley kept her mouth shut as they entered the house and just gave Elle the space to continue. She'd learned that much about Elle—she did things in her own time.

When they reached the kitchen, Elle finally continued, "The Petersons are going to be in LA this weekend and thought maybe we could meet for lunch Sunday, but I don't know. Mom was always so adamant that we should stay away from them. She would say letting them in was opening a window to them wanting more time with Luci, and then who knows? Maybe they would even want partial custody or something."

Ashley clicked on the stove to reheat the sauce for their dinner while Elle filled a pot with water for the pasta. Janet and her husband had to be in their sixties at least. Would people that age really try to gain custody of a teenager they'd never even met? Maybe there was reason to fear they would try that when Luci was a baby, but now? That didn't make sense.

"Okay, breathe a minute here. Do you think maybe it's just as straightforward as it's being presented?" Ashley suggested gently as she grabbed flatware to set the table. "Two people who lost their son and want to meet his child just to catch a glimpse of him and see what a beautiful young woman she's grown into? Because I don't think it's that hard to believe they would be curious about her. It seems totally normal. And maybe Luci's curious about them too."

"I guess," Elle agreed as she began to grate a block of parmesan cheese. "Maybe one lunch with them would be okay. If Luci wanted to do it. I'll think about it. But in the meantime, I have a proposition for you."

"A *proposition*?" Ashley teased. Elle was clearly changing the subject, but that was okay. She'd given her opinion, what happened next with the Petersons was up to Elle. "That certainly sounds fancy."

"I want it to be fancy. I want to take you out tomorrow night to celebrate our return to the *Celebrity Cook Off* kitchen. We'll get dressed up and have a nice dinner that we don't have to cook for a change. You know, a proper date."

She was right, they had been working so hard all week. They deserved a night to relax and celebrate. Not to mention, a date with Elle sounded wonderful. "I'm in. But I'm not wearing sensible shoes. If I'm going on a proper date, I'm wearing proper heels."

"It's a deal." Elle smiled. "I mean, it's a date."

CHAPTER FOURTEEN

Elle sipped her chardonnay and gazed out the floor-to-ceiling windows at the sapphire sea. It was the same vibrant blue as Ashley's eyes. She loved this view almost as much as she loved getting lost in those eyes. She owed Marigold big time for pulling the strings that got them a seaside table at Strand, one of the hottest dining spots on the coast, and at such short notice.

"I told you the menu would blow your mind." She grinned across the table. "What looks good to you?"

"I can't believe all the farm-fresh choices. Based on the location I thought it was going to be all seafood. I actually think I'm going to try the spaghetti-squash lasagna," Ashley said, trailing a well-manicured finger down the menu as if she wasn't one hundred percent certain of her decision. Elle couldn't blame her—there wasn't a bad selection in the bunch.

"I'm going with the skirt-steak burrito." She leaned in. "It's my favorite."

"And I can't believe this view." Ashley gestured at the window. They both stared for a moment at a dreamy-looking yacht with a white billowing sail. "So tranquil and mesmerizing. The way the sun sparkles on the water will never get old to me. I'm such a California girl at heart. I think it's one of the most beautiful things in the world."

Their gazes met once again and Elle reached across the table to take Ashley's hand. She was pretty sure she was looking at one of the other most beautiful things in the world. Before she could say as much, the moment was interrupted.

"What do we have here?" Mason Getty's unwelcome sneering tenor taunted. "Could it possibly be two competitors, or dare I say *rivals*, enjoying a romantic rendezvous on this summer's night? Are you two on a date or something?"

Elle pressed her lips tightly together biting back a smart-ass retort. Why was this guy such a jerk? They had no reason to hide the fact that they were on a date. There were no rules on the show regarding contestants fraternizing outside of the studio. God, Mason was such a jagoff. She wanted to tell him as much, but biting her tongue was just good manners while in a fancy restaurant on a date. She was on good behavior for Ashley.

"We are in fact on a date, Mason," Ashley said, seeming to force a smile like maybe if they had a moment of polite conversation he would move along. She looked uncomfortable, and Elle fought the urge to jump in and save her. Ashley wasn't some kind of damsel in distress, even if Elle did want to play the part of the hero in front of her.

Mason's bleached eyebrow arched up and he smirked. "Maybe I could join in with you two lovely ladies."

Disgust twisted Ashley's features and her jaw dropped, clearly at a loss for words at Mason's misguided suggestion. That was it. Time for Elle to shut it down.

"Mason, isn't there a boy band somewhere in need of your falsetto?" she quipped. "Better run along back to your boys."

He put a hand to his chest in mock shock. "So feisty. Wait, is this one of those reality TV alliances I've heard so much about? Yes, let's roll with this. I like the idea of the two of you taking me on. Very sexy."

"Goodbye, Mason," Elle and Ashley both said at the same time.

"Your loss." He shrugged. "But if you change your minds, I'll be at the bar."

They both gave him a hard stare until he gave up and walked away.

"He is not my favorite coworker," Ashley confessed before blowing out a long breath.

"Ash, I don't think Mason is anybody's favorite coworker." Elle laughed and took another sip of wine. "Guys like that mostly say that crap just to get a rise out of people. They want a reaction. It's up to you whether or not you're going to give them that satisfaction."

"I might give him a slap across the face, but believe you me, I have no intention of giving Mason any kind of satisfaction." Ashley shook her head before a teasing smile returned to her beautiful lips. "But I do like that your advice kind of rhymes. Reaction and satisfaction."

"Hey, the rhyme helps it stick." Elle pinched a piece of bread from a slice in the basket and lobbed it in Ashley's direction. To hell with good behavior. She was relieved that the dark cloud that had settled over the table had lifted. "How about this one, don't let Mason make you sick, just 'cause he's acting like a dick."

Ashley's big blue eyes went wide with surprise before she burst out in laughter so melodious Elle couldn't help but join in.

After a delicious dinner featuring easy conversation and a lot more laughter, Elle took Ashley down to the beach. They abandoned their shoes and walked down in the cool, dry sand to the water's edge. The ocean splashed cold over their feet and ankles, and they squealed and hopped in the surf. The moonlight reflecting on the dark water was the perfect backdrop for a romantic stroll. Elle took Ashley's hand and led her along the beach.

"You know, when I was young I was a total beach bum, so I totally get why Luci loves hanging out here," Elle said, swinging their hands between them. The night felt so perfect, she wanted it to stretch out forever like the ocean to the horizon. "If you stay away from it too long the feeling kinda fades. But the minute I hear the roar of the surf, and feel the sand between my toes, it all comes rushing back."

"Were you a surfer too?"

"I did okay with a boogie board, but that was about the extent of it." Elle glanced over at Ashley. The moonlight brought out glittering flecks of silver in her eyes. "I liked to swim and tan. Maybe throw around the frisbee for a bit. I could never do what Luci does."

"She's an amazing kid. You must be so proud of her."

She nodded, touched by Ashley's kind words about her daughter. That was something she'd never had in a romantic relationship before—she'd never let anyone in enough to get to know Luci. Friends, sure. Marigold spent time with Luci all the time. But not anyone Elle had actually slept with. "She's my whole world. You should see her on her board out there. She's totally awesome."

They walked in silence for a moment while the wind kicked up around them. Goose bumps rose on Elle's arms, but she was enjoying her night and wasn't quite ready to turn back.

"Speaking of Luci," Ashley said cautiously. "What did you decide about the Petersons? Did you email Janet back?"

Elle blew out a long breath. She'd been wrestling with this decision since she first opened Janet's message. She wanted to be honest with Ashley, but it was difficult to discuss the subject with someone who didn't know the whole story. Elle had lost the only other person who knew it—her mother. Ash was patiently waiting for Elle's response, letting her make the decision to share or not. Patience was one of the qualities Elle admired most in her. She'd witnessed it in many of those old episodes of her TV show. Over the past few weeks she'd proven she was patient as a friend too. And she was trustworthy. Elle was certain of that.

"You know, Josh Peterson and I were never a couple. We were just friends. I knew back when I was on *Sugar and Spice* with him that I was attracted to women, not men, but I was sixteen and there wasn't a lot of LGBT representation in the media. Hell, *The L Word* was only a season or two in back then. The other girls I hung out with were always talking about boys and sex and I just wanted to see what all the fuss was about. One night after filming we were partying with some of the other cast members and we just…" She shrugged and let Ashley fill in the blank. "Turns out what they say is true—it only takes one time. When I found out I was pregnant I told my mom before I told Josh. And then when told him, he wasn't all that pleased. I wanted to keep the baby, but he didn't. He was just about to turn twenty and he said he had his whole damn life in front of him. He didn't want a baby messing that up. I made it clear I didn't want anything from Josh, and I intended to raise the baby myself. My mom, God bless her, she supported my decision, and I knew I could count on her to help me. Less than a week after I told Josh I was pregnant he was written off the show. Right in the middle of the season. It felt so random. Then he overdosed and he was gone. It was tragic and horrible, and my mom was so afraid that even though he had no interest in the baby, his parents might. She insisted that we avoid them at all costs. She wouldn't even let me go to his funeral."

"Oh, Elle, I'm sorry." Ashley gave her hand a tender squeeze. "I'm sure she was scared and just trying to look after you, but that must've been so hard for you to not be able to say goodbye."

"It was, but I figured Mom knew best. She was my mom and my manager. I trusted her with everything." Elle shrugged. "With Josh gone and me too pregnant to film, they ended up canceling *Sugar and Spice* after that season. I lay low, cooked a lot with my mom, and nine months later, Luci entered our lives. I haven't looked back since. I didn't hear a word from the Petersons until I got the email after my mom passed. I never would have dreamed that they would reach out to me."

Ashley stopped walking and turned to face her. "So why now?"

"I don't know," Elle admitted. "Maybe it's one of those *we're not getting any younger* things. Mom was so involved in Luci's life. I can't imagine what it would've been like for her to never have known her granddaughter."

Ashley reached up and tucked a stray tendril of hair behind Elle's ear. "Maybe you should give the Petersons the chance to know her too."

The wind kicked up again, this time blowing sand against their legs. The moonlight hit the water. It was time to head back. Elle shivered and pulled Ashley to her. "I think you're right. If Luci is agreeable to the meeting I'll email Janet and see if Sunday still works. Can you do Sunday?"

Ashley's brow furrowed in confusion. "You want me to come with you?"

Elle chewed on her bottom lip. She knew it was a big ask, but she felt a lot more confident about agreeing to the meeting if she knew she would have Ash by her side. "Yeah. Would you do that?"

Ashley's expression softened. "Of course I will."

She dipped her head down and kissed Ashley's lips. It was a gentle, tender kiss that warmed her from head to toe.

"I would very much like to continue doing this," Ashley said with a grin as their lips parted. "But I think we should take it inside. There's definitely a storm blowing in."

"You're right again." Elle grabbed her hand and they started back. "While I'm confessing things from the past, I...I think I owe you an apology."

"You owe me an apology?" Ashley tipped her head and regarded her. Her lips pursed into a heart shape. So damn kissable. "What for?"

"When Luci was about six months old, they called me in for the *Canyon High* part. They actually asked for me. And I missed working so badly. I was over the moon, but my mom thought it was a terrible idea. She was worried about me going back to work while I had a new baby. She didn't want me dragging Luci to the set, but I didn't want to leave her while I was gone for long periods of filming. It was the only time me and Mom ever butted heads. In the end it didn't matter because, as you know, the studio decided a teen mom wasn't an image they wanted associated with Bailey Parker."

"But the wholesome, girl-next-door image Jill was pushing for me was." Ashley finished the thought for her. "So I got the role."

Elle nodded. At least Ashley hadn't denied it. "Back then I was resentful and jealous, and I realize now I've held on to those feelings for too long. I was the one who got pregnant. I was, in fact, a teen mom. That wasn't what the studio wanted. That's not your fault."

Ashley's chin tipped up as she gazed over at Elle, and the moon illuminated her sad eyes and the shame etched on her face.

"I'm ashamed to say that back then I would've done anything for that role," said Ashley. "I figured it was my big break and getting it was worth any price. But as time rolled on, I thought a lot about how childish and horrible it was to exploit your pregnancy to further my career. I'm the one who owes *you* an apology. I truly am sorry for the way you were treated."

"You were awesome as Bailey. Seriously, if I couldn't fill the role, I'm glad it was you." They'd reached their shoes again, but neither of them moved to put them back on their feet.

"That had to be such a hard time for you. You were a new mom with all those hormones coursing through you. Then you had to give up something you really loved." Ashley cupped her palm on Elle's cheek. "I hate that I had any part in making that even harder."

Elle dug a toe in the cool sand. "It was a long time ago, and we were both kids. The thing is, I think I was still holding on to that grudge when we started on *Celebrity Cook Off* and you didn't deserve that. I'm sorry. Can we just admit we both made childish mistakes and let it go?"

Ashley dropped her hands to her side and seemed to study Elle's face. "Of course we can. As soon as you answer one question." The corners of her mouth tipped upward, and her eyes twinkled with something that looked a lot like teasing. She laced their fingers. "Is that what all that weirdness about your top-secret chili recipe was about that first day on set?"

"Well, that and I don't share my chili recipe with just anyone," Elle teased back before stealing a quick kiss.

"And now that you've gotten to know me, maybe you feel more comfortable sharing that recipe."

"Has this whole thing between us just been a ruse to get your hands on my chili recipe?" Elle feigned shock. "I did not see this coming."

Ashley grabbed her hips and pulled her close. "I want my hands on something tonight, but it's not your chili recipe."

A shiver that had nothing to do with the wind worked its way down Elle's spine. "Grab your shoes, Ash. I can't wait to get you home. And you can put your hands wherever you want."

CHAPTER FIFTEEN

Ashley woke up content on Saturday morning, naked, warm, and comfortable in Elle's arms. Their romantic dinner and walk on the beach had led to a night of delicious lovemaking back in Elle's bedroom. Even now, wrapped up in the sheets with the morning sun peeking through the edges of the window around the vertical blinds, her body hummed with the memory of the kisses, touches, and pure bliss that had lasted late into the night.

When Elle apologized to her on the beach, Ashley had been caught off guard. She wasn't surprised Elle had held a grudge all these years. She could easily understand why she felt that way. Teenage Hollywood was a cutthroat business and the rush of being a bright star in that universe was a hell of a drug. Ashley could still remember those feelings clearly, but those years were in the past for them. The part she found surprising was how honest Elle was with her. It was brave to admit you knew you'd behaved badly and you were ashamed. To give a raw, honest, heartfelt apology. Elle didn't have to say anything, but she did the right thing. That's what struck Ashley the most.

Behind her, Elle rustled out of slumber. Their hips bumped and her breath was warm against Ashley's neck. "Morning."

Ashley rolled over to face her. The freshly awake version of Elle was adorable. Her sleepy brown eyes blinking to adjust to the light, her cheek creased from extended contact with the pillowcase. She wished they could stay snuggled up in the bed together all day, just lie there in each other's arms, but Luci would be home from her sleepover soon. Ashley couldn't linger. "Morning. What have you got planned for the day?"

"Mmm." Elle slid a hand between Ashley's thighs. "How about a little bit of this?"

The touch made Ashley's pulse race and she felt a familiar tug in her middle. Morning sex sounded heavenly. Elle's teenage daughter walking in on them did not. She wiggled her hips out of Elle's reach. "I don't think we have time for that. Luci could be home any minute."

"I've been pressed up against a very sexy woman for the past few hours. I probably only need a minute."

Ashley laughed and trailed her fingertips down Elle's arm, but she kept that safe distance between them to help fight temptation. "I know how that will go. One minute will lead to two, and two will lead to three…"

"And so on, and so on," Elle completed the thought and blew out a long breath. "Yeah, I know. You're right. So, what's our plan B?"

Ashley sighed and rolled onto her back. "I guess I should get dressed and head out. Do you mind if I hop in the shower really quick?"

Elle sat up beside her. "I don't mind you showering, but I'm not wild about the heading out part. Why don't you stick around a while?"

"Oh, no. I don't want to impose." Ashley kicked her legs out of the sheets and over the edge of the bed. "Plus I need to get in some kind of workout today."

"I'd say you got in a pretty damn good workout last night." Elle smirked, but when Ashley hit her with a withering look she sobered. "Fine. We could go for a run. A little exercise wouldn't hurt me either. We'll spend the day together just relaxing for a change. Then we'll make some dinner."

Ashley didn't really want to leave, but there was something holding her back from agreeing to stay, and she wasn't sure how to broach the subject with Elle. It was easier just to take a break, go home, and reconvene later. "Elle, I don't have any workout clothes here and besides, if I stay until after dinner I'll just be going home to sleep then turning back around to be here to head out for lunch with Luci and the Petersons. It's silly."

"Yes," Elle agreed. "It is silly. You might as well stay the whole weekend. We're just about the same size and I've got a whole closet full of clothes. You can help yourself to whatever you want."

"No, I couldn't..." She stood and stepped away from the bed. Maybe a little more distance would make this easier. "I mean, I don't think I should."

Elle rolled out of bed and took her in her arms, peppering kisses on her neck. Making leaving even harder. "I'm not asking you to move in permanently, just stay for the weekend." More kisses making leaving nearly impossible. "I like waking up next to you."

"I like it too, but..." Ashley knew excuses weren't going to cut it. Elle had been brave when she'd been honest about her feelings on the beach. She needed to be honest about what was holding her back now. "But what will Luci think?"

Elle didn't let go of her, but her arms went slack like she'd lost some of her moxie. "What are you talking about? Luci likes you."

"No, I know that. But what will she think about me staying here—taking up space in your house—sleeping in her mother's bed? She's not a little kid. I'm sure she knows what that means."

Elle pulled back to look at her. "Yes, she does know what that means. I've talked openly and honestly about sex with my daughter from the moment she was old enough to hear it. But I can promise you that sex is not going to be where her mind goes when she learns you're going to stay the weekend. What she's going to think is, it's about damn time that her mother found some happiness." She pushed a strand of hair off Ashley's face. "Because you make me very, very happy."

Warmth flooded Ashley from head to toe. She pulled Elle to her again, pressing their bare breasts together, and kissed her hard and urgently. "I'm very, very happy to hear that. Because I intend to continue making you happy."

"You're also making me very horny," Elle said, digging her fingers into Ashley's butt cheeks.

"Oh no." She squirmed out of grasp. "I'll stay, but we are keeping this weekend totally PG-13."

Elle raised her hands in surrender but gave a wink. "Whatever it takes."

"Well, don't worry, I have the perfect project to keep us on track with that."

"Oh, a project!" Elle waggled her eyebrows. "What did you have in mind?"

"I've had my eye on your busted-up firepit for weeks. Today's the day we tackle it."

After a hearty omelet breakfast, the women took Elle's El Camino to the local hardware store where Ashley encouraged her to select pavers with a little more style than the cement blocks that previously made up the pit. It didn't take long to clear out the old rubble and get started with the new.

"Luckily, now that we've got it down to the gravel, we can build on that. It looks like you had a nice, level base." Ashley was relieved to see they wouldn't have to start from square one, although she had been prepared to do whatever was needed to get the project done properly. "Our first step is to lay the first row in place. Make sure all the stones are touching, like this." She set three of the pavers in a curve.

"Makes sense," Elle said, taking a turn lining up pavers. "Gotta have a good base to build upon. Like the first layer of a trifle or lasagna."

Ashley couldn't hold back her giggle. "Do you ever stop thinking about food?" she teased.

"You know, I really don't."

They worked together staggering the second row of pavers, using landscape adhesive to secure them firmly in place, and then they repeated the process. It took both of them to lift and reinsert the metal pit ring, but they did it. And just like that, the firepit was done. They stood back and admired their work.

"We did it!" Elle grabbed Ashley's hand and reeled her in close for a kiss. "You are an absolute home improvement champ! I still can't believe you know how to do all this stuff."

"I like doing it." Ashley shrugged like it was nothing, but her chest filled with pride. She adored a good project, and she'd always been the one to handle home maintenance issues since David had been so darn hopeless on the subject. Lately she'd been aching to do more of it. An idea had started taking hold in her mind, and she'd been wanting to run it by Elle. While they were both high on their latest success was probably a good time to bring it up. "Elle, there's something I want to do, but I need your help."

"Is it something sexy?"

"Not during our PG-13 weekend. But I definitely don't want to do this with anyone but you."

"I'm intrigued." Elle tipped her head to the side and regarded her. "Go on."

She took a deep breath. This was the first time she'd spoken the idea out loud. "I want to write a book using your recipes and my home-improvement projects all tied together with some of those beautiful food pics you post on Insta—I'm hoping you can take some of my projects too—and collection of essays and anecdotes about growing up and continuing our careers into adulthood. Two Hollywood kids turned Hollywood adults, making a fulfilling life in La La Land, you know?"

When the words stopped tumbling out of her mouth, Ashley finally dared to meet Elle's gaze. To her relief Elle's surprised expression quickly morphed into a smile.

"You write?" Elle asked. Her forehead was shiny with the sweat of their work and it made the baby-fine wisps of hair framing her face curl. She probably hated that. Ashley tried to ignore how cute it was.

"I've kept a journal since I was a kid. It's been a little more sporadic since my life has become a reality TV show, but those precious quiet moments at the break of dawn when you're awake before the camera crew arrives and the coffee is steaming in your mug can be quite inspiring. I figure there's plenty of material in the numerous notebooks I've filled over the years."

"Just when I think I know you…" Elle squinted her eyes in a piercing gaze that seemed to pin Ashley in place. It sent a shiver of excitement through her.

"I like to keep you on your toes." Ashley's cheeks warmed with something more than the flush from wrestling pavers. *Focus.* "But back to the idea—what do you think?"

"I think it's brilliant."

"Really?"

"Really." Elle nodded enthusiastically. "I think we should do it. I'm in."

Ashley's heart soared. Why had she been so worried about approaching Elle? If anyone was going to support her idea, of course it would be her. She threw her arms around her neck. "Thank you."

"Of course, Ash." Elle's breath tickled her neck. "It's really a great idea."

Before their celebration could push the boundaries of a PG-13 rating, Luci joined them in the backyard.

"Mom! Mom, I can't decide if I should wear my new pink skirt, or my white shorts and the tie-dyed tank I bought last week." Luci had been talking nonstop about their plans to meet the Petersons. Although it seemed to be a mixture of nervousness and excitement, it was definitely positive, and Ashley was happy for her and Elle. And even for the Petersons. She couldn't imagine how it felt for them all to be reconnecting after all this time.

"Hmmm." Elle scrunched up her face like she was really thinking about it. "That's a real headscratcher, Lu."

"I really like your pink skirt," Ashley mused. "Have you ever paired it with that blush-toned twist-front top? That might look really striking together."

"Oh my gosh!" Luci squealed. "That would be perfect. I'm gonna go try it now. I'm so glad you're coming with us tomorrow, Ashley," she called over her shoulder, already on her way to her room.

"How do you do that?" Elle shook her head and picked up the trash from the firepit overhaul.

"What?"

"That kid has never taken a single stitch of wardrobe advice from me. You suggest one combination and she can't get to her closet fast enough."

Ashley laughed. Without a doubt she and Elle had different styles. She'd spent the morning wearing a pair of loose-fit denim capris that cuffed just below the knee and a black V-neck T-shirt out of Elle's closet. It wasn't her usual look, but the shirt held enough of Elle's scent to set off butterflies in her stomach anytime Ashley caught a whiff of it. What was with the hold this woman had on her? She'd actually put her face to the shirt and sniffed it earlier when Elle wasn't looking. "I'm new here. You know how teenagers are—they like anything new. I'm probably a passing fancy. From what I've heard, teenagers are pretty fickle too."

Elle dropped the trash bag and pulled Ashley into her arms. "You're wonderful and I can promise you—you're no passing fancy to me. You're so good with Luci. I really appreciate that."

"She's a pleasure—such a good kid. And she's got a big heart, just like you." When Elle shot her a doubtful look she continued, "Oh, please. Everybody who meets you loves you."

"I don't know about that," Elle sighed, and sank into one of the Adirondack chairs surrounding the pit.

"No, it's true," Ashley insisted. After all, she'd become quite fond of her in the short time they'd been working together, but she wasn't quite ready to announce those feelings. There were plenty of other examples she could offer up. "The people at the farmers' market, Nan at the women's shelter, Rocco and company."

"Not the people we're having lunch with tomorrow."

"Ah. This is about the Petersons." Ashley settled in on the arm of the chair. Seeing Elle anything less than confident was disturbing. "You're nervous."

"I hate to admit it, but I am. My mom really drilled that fear into me. I know deep down that the Petersons probably just want to meet Luci, but I can't help it, my mama-bear instinct is so damn strong. I'd do anything to keep her safe."

"Hey." Ashley grabbed Elle's hand and brought it to her lips, gently kissing her knuckles. "Of course you would. You're a good mom. That's what good moms do—protect their babies. But everything will be okay. We'll have some lunch, they'll get to visit with your amazing daughter, and then it will be over. And I'll be right by your side the whole time."

"Thank you," Elle whispered.

"Always," Ashley whispered back.

CHAPTER SIXTEEN

Elle laced up her high-top Converse sneakers and folded the hem of her jeans into neat cuffs. She'd felt extra fussy all morning—taking time to straighten her hair and put on a fresh coat of nail polish. She'd even changed her shirt three times before deciding on a vintage Roxy Music tee.

"You look beautiful," Ashley said, grabbing her shoulders from behind and giving them a rub. "It's one lunch. You can do this."

"It's not me I'm worried about. It's Luci. Maybe this meeting was a bad idea."

"What was a bad idea?" Luci breezed into the living room obviously ready to go to lunch. She was wearing the outfit she and Ashley had picked out and accessorized with a cute floral print crossbody cell-phone bag.

From the second Elle had mentioned the meeting with the Petersons, Luci had been agreeable. She seemed to frame meeting her biological grandparents in scientific terms. Did she look like them? Did they like the beach too? Were either of them left-handed like she was. Much more curious about the facts than the feelings.

That didn't surprise Elle. She and Luci had watched all the old *Sugar and Spice* episodes together. Luci understood Josh had a substance use disorder and died from an overdose. There were some stories from her time with Josh on the set that Elle shared with Luci, but her daughter also knew they hadn't been an actual couple. Elle didn't know his favorite color, or if he liked to read, or even his medical history. Maybe she should make a list of scientific questions for the Petersons too.

"No, nothing. No bad ideas here," Elle said as she shrugged into her jacket. "Everything is totally fine. It's just that…if you don't feel like going today we can still cancel. We can just call and say, 'nope, we are not gonna show up.' Easy as that."

"Mom! Mom, everything *is* totally fine. If we like the Petersons, then great, we met cool people. If they turn out to be jerks, then we don't have to see them ever again. It's that simple." She fiddled with the strap of the bag on her shoulder. "Come on, we're gonna be late."

"Smart kid," Ashley whispered, linking her arm through Elle's as they followed Luci out the door.

"Maybe she gets that from the Petersons," Elle cracked.

"I think she gets it from you." Ashley kissed her on the cheek before they dropped hands to go to their separate sides of the El Camino. And off they went.

Elle sat at the outdoor café across the table from Timothy and Janet Peterson and sipped her iced tea, surprised that she was enjoying the afternoon. Janet was friendly, if initially a little reserved, but she seemed to take to Luci instantly, plying her with compliments and asking her endless questions about her life. Luci did her part, happily chattering away about school and surfing.

As Timothy described the daily routine caring for the animals on their alpaca farm just outside Fresno, Elle leaned back in her chair. Her sense of dread at the beginning of this meeting had finally dissipated. They had made it to dessert. The reunion was nearly over. Elle had done the kind thing, let the Petersons meet their granddaughter, and survived. Luci certainly seemed none the worse for wear. Elle bumped her knee against Ashley's under the table, telegraphing her relief. The quick wink Ash gave in response evidenced her acknowledgment and gave Elle a bubbly feeling.

"Alpacas are so cute," Luci gushed, squinting at the pictures on Timothy's phone. "Maybe some time I can come see them in person."

"You ladies are welcome to visit any time." Timothy beamed, obviously proud of his farm. He had a very down-home, salt-of-the-earth thing about him that Elle was drawn to immediately. She could picture him tending the alpacas, talking to them in his gentle voice, calling each of them their special name.

"Absolutely," Janet agreed, signaling their server for the check by making a little checkmark sign with her hand in the air. At least she hadn't snapped her fingers at him. "This is our treat, by the way. We're just so thrilled to finally be able to get together with you and meet Luci after all these years."

Was it a dig to guilt Elle, or just an honest statement? She didn't know Janet well enough to know, and it didn't matter anyway. What was done was done. She had made her choices based on what she and her mother believed was best for Luci, and there was nothing wrong with that. She forced a smile. "It was so nice to finally meet you both. It's just a shame we waited so long that my mom missed out on meeting you. I think you would've gotten along."

Janet's expression soured like a rotten lemon and Timothy put a protective arm around her. "Oh no, dear. We made it a point to wait to reach out until she had passed. I never wanted to see that woman again. She's the reason we lost our Joshua."

Elle choked on her tea. "Excuse me? She's the *what*?"

"If she hadn't had Joshua fired from his show, he never would have spiraled the way he did." Janet's mouth twisted into an ugly scowl and tears suddenly rimmed her eyes. She aged ten years in an instant. "Losing his part on *Sugar and Spice* was more than he could bear. My poor, sweet boy."

"Come on, honey," Timothy cajoled. The same voice he probably used with the alpacas. "We've had such a pleasant afternoon."

Ashley whispered something to Luci who promptly slipped away from the table and ambled down the sidewalk toward the bookstore they'd spotted on their way in. Elle's pulse was pounding in her ears, making her wonder if perhaps she had misheard, or at least misunderstood what Janet had said. "You think my mom had Josh fired from *Sugar and Spice*?"

"Oh, I don't think, dear. I *know*." Janet's teary eyes had now gone steely. "When you got pregnant she told the producers that he'd preyed on you, the sweet, young star, and took advantage of you. He was almost twenty years old and you were a minor. She didn't want him anywhere near you and threatened to report him to the police and make it public that he was the father if they didn't get him off the set. That was all it took. Those asshole producers were much more afraid of a sex scandal than the consequences of firing their male lead. And you know what happened to him after he was written off the show. It's impossible not to believe those two things were connected."

When she got pregnant? Like Elle was the only party involved in the event? Elle bit the inside of her cheek. Could actual steam be coming out of her burning ears? Was this woman for real?

Ashley grabbed Elle's hand, either to remind her she was there, or to keep her from jumping across the table and throttling Janet Peterson. It was hard for Elle to be sure, but she appreciated the touch anyway.

"I...I don't believe you." Elle shook her head, trying to force away the burning sensation in her ears. "My mom had nothing to do with Josh being written off the show."

Janet's laugh was a low, bitter tremble that sounded like she'd perfected it over the years. "You've got connections in Hollywood. Ask around. You'll find out the truth. Your mother as good as killed my son. The father of your baby."

"That's a lie." Elle jumped to her feet. "And I'm not going to sit here while you speak ill of my mother like that. She was right about you all along. You're a horrible person."

She didn't wait for a rebuttal. She grabbed her phone from the table and stalked off, pulling Ashley along with her. Leaving the Petersons behind for good.

They'd made it a block before Ashley finally spoke. "What the hell was that? What was she talking about?"

"What a bitch! I mean, who says something like that?" Elle squeezed her temples. Her head was pounding with rage. "Sure, my mom wasn't exactly thrilled when she found out Josh was the father of the baby, but to have him fired from the show? No. That couldn't be right. Once he had made it clear he didn't want anything to do with the baby, Mom just kind of pretended like he didn't exist. It was just the three of us against the world from that point on."

She scrubbed a hand over her face as they stopped in front of the bookstore. "It doesn't make any sense. And it's really crappy for Janet to say that when Mom isn't even here anymore to defend herself."

Ashley said nothing but put a comforting arm around Elle's shoulders. The touch was a balm to Elle's frayed nerves. Through the store window Elle could see Luci approaching the register, a couple of books in her hands. Good sense returned to Elle.

"Janet said if I asked around I'd find out the truth. Maybe I should do that," she said as she waved at her daughter through the window. The idea was picking up steam in her mind. "Jill was your agent back then, right? She knew my mother. I could ask her."

Concern troubled Ashley's pretty face. "I don't know, Elle. That could have just been bluster from a sad woman still grieving the loss of her son."

"No." She was set on this course and she wasn't going to change her mind. "Janet said those lies in front of Luci. Lies about Luci's grandmother. I at least owe it to Mom to clear her name for Luci."

Ashley's gaze darted to Luci walking toward the bookstore's exit before settling back on Elle. "If that's what you want, we can talk to Jill. But you know your mom. You know how dedicated she was to you and Luci. You have nothing to prove."

The bell above the door jingled as Luci stepped out onto the sidewalk, smiling and proudly holding up her purchase. "So, the Petersons turned out to be jerks, but at least I got some new books!"

Luci seemed none the worse for wear, but still Elle couldn't shake the feeling that she had to clear her mother's good name. If a little chat with Jill was what it would take, then that's what she would do.

CHAPTER SEVENTEEN

On set that Monday, the competition was back on track and more heated than ever. Production kicked off with the Stew Week episode that had been postponed when Benji had his salmonella incident. Ashley hoped to dazzle the judges with her beef bourguignon.

The whole *Cook Off* kitchen seemed happy to be back in action. The contestants were buzzing with excitement, and Ashley was feeling the vibe. She even hummed a cheerful tune as she chopped carrots and mushrooms.

"You're sure in a good mood." Elle sidled up to her workstation. The fresh apple blossom scent of Elle's shampoo had become something of a comfort to Ashley in the past few days. How could it not? When she stayed over at Elle's house the scent surrounded her. In Elle's bed sheets, her bath towels, the Champion hoodie Ashley had borrowed and still not returned.

"I've made it through two elimination rounds and I'm feeling good about today's challenge. It's like some kind of culinary miracle. What's not to be in a good mood about?"

"It's not *some kind of culinary miracle*." Elle leaned in and her warm breath tickled Ashley's neck. "You've worked hard and actually learned to cook. Turns out you're pretty damn good at it too. You've earned your spot here."

A shiver worked down Ashley's spine. Elle's chest pressed into her back, and a blast of endorphins shot off inside her. This woman had a hell of an effect on her. "Are you trying to distract me from making my delicious bourguignon?"

"Certainly not," Elle said as she slid one hand down Ashley's hip. Definitely distracting. "I just thought I'd come over and say hello."

God, she didn't want to, but Ashley wiggled her way out of Elle's grasp. They'd made a plan and, damn it, as hard as it felt in that moment, she was going to stick to it. She spun and pointed a flour-covered finger. "We are supposed to be lying low on set and you feeling up my ass is not lying low."

Elle's laugh was quiet and throaty and she held up her open palms in surrender. "Okay, okay. We won't let anyone know that we're…" She leaned in again and stage-whispered, "Lovers."

"Get out of here!" Ashley laughed and gave her a playful shove that left a white smudge of flour on Elle's black Blondie concert T-shirt. "I've got work to do and you do too. The clock's ticking, you know. Don't you have your own stew to…stew?"

Elle was making cassoulet, a classic French stew—her mother's recipe, of course. Her dish made with chicken, pork, mutton and a specialized sausage, saucisse de Toulouse, required a perfect slow cook to come out just right.

"The veggies and cannellini beans are already happily simmering away on the stovetop." Elle smirked. "I've got the remaining three and a half hours planned down to the second. I'm simply taking a coffee break."

That teasing smirk made Ashley's nipples go insta-hard. A Pavlovian response. In the past few days that teasing smirk had led to mind-blowing sexy times on several occasions. But she didn't have the same culinary confidence as Elle, and she needed every minute of cooking time. She needed to get back to her own dish, and that meant sending Elle back to her own workstation. "Then go get your coffee. Or get back to your beans. Just…get."

"There you go giving orders in the kitchen again. You know I like that." Elle winked before turning and sauntering off toward Benji's workspace. More socializing. That woman was something else.

Ashley turned her attention to getting her russet potatoes into the pot to make the mash to accompany her beef bourguignon. Boiling them whole with their skins on would take a little longer, but since the potatoes would absorb less water that way, the results would be worth it. She had just plopped the last one into the pot and put the lid on when the former NFL star Michael Taylor casually strolled into her space.

"You're serving your stew over mashed potatoes instead of egg noodles?" he asked, squinting and pursing his lips, apparently doubting her vision for the dish. He leaned his hefty form against the countertop and crossed his legs at the ankles, settling in for a conversation. Didn't these people have their own recipes to worry about? First Elle and now Michael? "My mom always served stew over egg noodles. That's old school. Everyone likes it, you know? Nothing like sitting down to watch football with a Sunday supper of beef stew over egg noodles."

"Egg noodles?" Ashley had never considered serving her dish over anything other than mashed potatoes. That was how Elle had taught her, so that was what she'd planned. She could probably make egg noodles from scratch since she'd made pasta with Elle before, but not now. "I can't change direction now. There's not enough time to make noodles from scratch. I have way too many other things to do."

"Just grab a bag of noodles from the pantry. No big deal."

Egg noodles from a bag? No. Too pedestrian. Anyway, she'd decided on potatoes, and she was sticking to that. "Michael, this is not just beef stew. It's beef bourguignon."

"Beef bourguignon," he repeated. His deep voice was as rich and comforting as a good stew. He nodded slowly. "Okay. Okay, Castle. But are you using cremini mushrooms or just the plain old white ones?"

Plain old white ones? As if! "Cremini."

"Okay, now he's just messing with you." Elle slipped back into Ashley's workstation. Seriously, was anybody else in the kitchen actually cooking? She swatted a tea towel playfully at him. "Get out of here and let the woman do her work."

Michael pushed off the counter and raised his hands in surrender, but before he walked away he tossed a teasing wink over his shoulder at Ashley.

When he was out of earshot, she grabbed Elle. "Do you think he's right? Does everyone love noodles with their beef stew?"

"You can do either noodles or mashed potatoes. That's up to you. But noodles from a bag?" Elle grimaced. "I just don't know how that will go over with the judges."

"That's exactly what I thought!"

"Sounds like your instincts are spot-on." Elle shrugged. "You should trust them."

Ashley followed her instincts and served her beef bourguignon over her mashed potatoes. But would the decision be the right one? Standing in front of the three-judge panel was always unnerving, and that feeling only increased with each round as they got closer to the final.

She stood with her hands clasped behind her back to still them while the judges sampled her offering. Had potatoes been a better choice than egg noodles? The moans of pleasure from the panel were encouraging, and Ashley forced herself not to bounce on her toes in anticipation of their final verdict.

Julie Marten, last season's winner of Eats! Chanel's *Next Big Cooking Thing* said, "This is the first time I've ever had beef bourguignon, and you've definitely made me a fan."

"You can tell a lot of thought and love went into the execution of this recipe." Anthony Centini waved his spoon as he spoke. The owner of Factory Fourteen restaurant and author of three cookbooks was known as the toughest judge of the group. "But I would like a little more sharpness to come through. A little more onion or garlic, I think. Something to give it a little more punch."

But it was Rosilee Nunez, star of Eats! Chanel's *You Can Cook It* who said what Ashley wanted to hear. "Your flavors were complex, and warm and comforting, but the element that really brought the dish home for me was your homemade mashed potatoes. They were buttery and wonderful, and honestly I wish I could just eat a whole plateful of them."

"Thank you, judges." Ashley felt like she could finally breathe again as she left the *Cook Off* kitchen to make way for the next contestant to face the panel. She'd followed her instincts and it had paid off. Success!

Elle's cassoulet was also a hit, securing her a spot in the next round as well. In the end it was former sitcom mom Joan Brandy who was eliminated that round after Anthony likened her mushy chicken and dumplings to papier-mâché before officially sending her packing.

"We live to see another day." Elle hooked her arm through Ashley's as they walked out of the studio. "And just in time to meet Jill."

Ashley wasn't as excited about the meeting. She still didn't think Elle had anything to prove, but she was doing her best to be supportive. "Are you sure about this? The whole thing might just be a story the Petersons made up to deal with the grief after losing their son."

"Believe me," Elle said as they climbed into the El Camino, "I know about grieving. I've been doing my share the past six months. That's exactly why I feel so strongly about this. They said that shit in front of Luci. I want to be able to tell her I confirmed it's a lie."

Ashley had nodded in agreement and reached across the console to squeeze Elle's hand.

Thirty minutes later when they were sharing a tall outdoor bar table overlooking the bay with Jill and ordering mojitos, Ashley knew the conversation was not going to go the way Elle had hoped.

Their drinks had barely been served when Elle got straight to the point. "Jill, it's probably no surprise that I'm not your biggest fan, but Ashley and I already rehashed all that *Canyon Rock High* stuff and agreed to move on. I have a couple of questions for you and I would very much appreciate some honest answers."

Ashley nodded her support. It was time for her to speak up and be accountable for her part in what they'd done. "Jill, what we did back then—taking advantage of Elle being a teen mom—it was wrong. It's bothered me for years and I'm embarrassed now to admit I went along with it without a second thought. We shouldn't have done it."

"I couldn't agree more." Jill took a delicate sip of mojito. "I didn't want to do it back then, and I've never done anything like it since."

Elle's brow scrunched in confusion. "Then why did you?"

Ashley knew by the way Jill tapped her readers against the table that she was picking her words carefully. She'd seen her make that move a million times before. Strategically deciding what information to share.

"Your mother and I weren't exactly best friends, Elle. But we did float in the same circles," she began. "When you were offered the Bailey Parker role, she came to me and asked me to help her. She didn't want you to go back to work so soon after having your baby, and she had an idea. She thought that maybe if I went to the studio and put a bug in their ear about casting the part based on wholesome values or some such nonsense—provided them an alternative that would fill the bill—that they might rescind their offer to you."

Ashley nearly choked on her mojito. Hélène Bissett had asked Jill to start the campaign to take the role from Elle? This was news to her. She felt Elle's surprised gaze turn to her. "I had no idea about this," she whispered.

"My mom asked you to do it?" Elle was incredulous as she focused on Jill again. "That can't be true."

"I'm sorry, but it is." Jill shook her head. She clearly took no pleasure in revealing this secret from the past. "She just wanted you to be able to spend more time with your new baby."

"God, Mom, how could you?" Elle muttered before meeting Jill's gaze again. Defeat clouded her usually bright eyes. "I hate to even ask the question we came here to ask now, but I guess I need to know the truth. We had lunch with Josh Peterson's parents yesterday. His mom said my mother was the reason Josh was written off *Sugar and Spice*. She said she threatened to sue the show if they didn't fire him for getting me pregnant. Any chance this is just a load of crap?"

For the first time since Janet had confronted her, Elle's expression reflected doubt. There was a glimpse of fear. Like she was considering for the first time that maybe she was the one who'd had the story wrong all this time.

Ashley grabbed Elle's hand, wanting to fortify her for whatever was about to come. She nodded at Jill to let her know it was okay. If Elle didn't hear it from her, she would just continue to search. At least Ashley knew Jill could deliver rough news gently. God knew she'd done it plenty of times over the years after Ashley had auditioned unsuccessfully.

"I don't know if there was an actual threat to sue," Jill began slowly, pausing to take another sip of mojito and possibly think through the best way to answer. "But yes, after she found out Josh was the father of your baby, Hélène met with the producers of *Sugar and Spice* and the network people. She pointed out that their employee got a fellow employee, who happened to be a minor, pregnant and how that might not be the best look. Apparently, the network agreed. After that he was written off the show."

Elle blanched visibly and her hand went limp in Ashley's grasp.

"I know this isn't what you were expecting—or wanting—to hear. None of it," Jill continued gently. "Like I said, I knew your mother and she was a good woman. The way she went about these things might have been misguided, but she was only trying to protect her little girl."

Elle took a big swig of mojito as if she needed something to wash down the truth and keep it from sticking in her throat. She shook her head as she swallowed hard. "No, that can't be right. I just…that can't be right."

Ashley put her hand on Elle's bouncing knee. "Honey…"

"No, it's okay."

"I'm sorry," Jill said. "I know it's hard to hear, but that is what happened. You said you were looking for the truth."

"Really." Elle rubbed her hands over her face. She pushed her chair back and Ashley's hand fell from her knee. "I did ask for the truth, and I'm okay. It's fine."

"Elle, let me get you a glass of water." Ashley didn't like the way Elle's neck was turning crimson. It was like her body was filling up with red-hot anger and hurt.

"You don't have to do that." Elle pushed up from her chair. "I'm just going to go. I, uh…I need to kind of process this."

"I'll come with you," Ashley offered, reaching for her purse. Jill would understand.

"No," Elle said sharply, but her expression softened as her gaze met Ashley's. "I'm sorry. I need to be alone. I'll text you later."

As Elle turned to go, Ashley began to rise from her seat to follow, but Jill grabbed her arm, keeping her anchored in place.

"Let her have some space. She's had a shock," she said, nodding sagely. "She's right. She has to process. It's one thing to think something might possibly be true. It's a whole different ballgame when you actually confirm it."

"That's why she needs me." Ashley couldn't shake the look of hurt in Elle's eyes before she walked away.

"She just told you she needs to be alone." Jill released her grip on Ashley's arm and turned her attention back to her mojito, taking a delicate sip before continuing, "Instead of rushing off, take a minute and tell me how things went in the kitchen today."

The stew cook-off seemed like days ago. She'd been so proud of her performance, but now it hardly seemed to matter. She was so worried about Elle, and so shocked to learn all that Hélène had done. It felt like she had some processing of her own to do. Jill had made a good point though—Elle asked for space. Maybe that was the best thing Ashley could do for her in the moment. She took a drink and gave her mind a moment to settle. "Things went well. I made beef bourguignon and I'm through to the next round. So is Elle."

Jill looked incredulous. "You made beef bourguignon? Are you kidding me right now? The last time I was in your kitchen you could barely make a sandwich."

Ashley pulled a face at Jill's exaggeration, but she couldn't deny the vast improvement in her cooking skills in the past two weeks, and she knew exactly who was responsible for that. "It's all thanks to Elle. She really whipped me into shape with her cooking boot camp last week. She's amazing."

"I see." Jill seemed to study her face for a moment. "This is more than just some reality show fling, isn't it? You have some real feelings for this woman."

It was funny how Ashley had fallen into those feelings so naturally that it hadn't exactly struck her as a big change. It just sort of happened along the way. She nodded in answer to Jill's question. Elle had changed her life in the time they'd spent together, in and out of the kitchen. And it wasn't all about cooking either. Ashley's mind reeled back to that moment in the *Cook Off* kitchen earlier when Elle had pushed her to trust her intuition. Ashley had known what she wanted to do all along, even as Michael was goading her to make a last-minute audible to her game plan. Elle reminded her that her instincts were pushing her in a direction for a reason. It was all it took for Ashley to find the confidence to stick to her guns, or at least to her mashed potatoes.

Now her instincts were telling her that Elle wasn't having a diva moment. Elle needed Ashley with her for support and comfort.

"Elle is special to me," she said, standing and looping her purse over her shoulder. "And that's why I've got to go to her now. She's hurting and I should be there for her. I'm sorry to run, but I'll call you tonight to fill you in on the rest of the *Cook Off* stuff."

Jill waved her hands in the air. Bye-bye-bye. "Go get your woman."

CHAPTER EIGHTEEN

When Elle got home, she marched to the laundry room and opened the louvred doors opposite the washer and dryer. She faced the closet that had been closed for at least two years, the contents untouched and practically forgotten. Three shelves of boxes full of her mother's old files. If there were any answers to be found, they would be in this closet.

She tugged the box labeled "2006," the year she got pregnant, off the shelf and hauled it into the living room where the lighting was better. Her mom had kept everything—pay stubs, script sheets, tax crap—but nothing that gave Elle any insight into why Josh was fired from *Sugar and Spice* or whether or not her mother had really conspired with Jill on the *Canyon Rock High* casting. She didn't know exactly what it was she was looking for, or what difference it would make if she found anything anyway. All she knew was she had to find *something* solid. Some kind of factual evidence besides people's recollection of the past. Unfortunately, after pulling every sheet of paper from the box, she had nothing.

Leaving the papers scattered on the floor around the empty box, she returned to the closet for the "2007" box. Maybe the proof would show up in the year Luci was born. There were less pages to sort through in this one, but still nothing that told her what she needed to know. Desperation kicked in as she reached the bottom of that second box. She frantically sifted through the stacks of paper on the floor around her. There had to be some scrap of paper, some note or, God, even an old Post-it there that would give her some answers.

She could deal with the idea that her mother convinced Jill to push the wholesome Ashley agenda so she got the part instead of her. She knew her mother had wanted her to wait to go back to work so she could spend more time with her new baby. Even though losing the role had stung when she was a teen, she didn't regret that she had that time with Luci. But could her mother really have been the reason Josh got written off the show? It took two of them to get her pregnant. To Elle's way of thinking, it wasn't fair for anyone to blame him solely.

Her mind slipped back to the day she'd told her mother she was pregnant. Elle had been so nervous and scared, but she'd also been thrilled. From the minute she had found out, Elle could picture her life with a child. Sure, she was young and had no idea how to be a parent, but she could feel it in her bones— she was meant to raise that baby. And while her mother had looked like she was going to pass out when she first heard the news, once Elle had made her intentions clear, her mother had been nothing but supportive. She'd taught Elle how to do it all, from diapering and bathing baby Lucille to making homemade baby food. Once the new mother and baby came home from the hospital it was the three of them against the world. That was the exact phrase her mother would use back then. Did she take it so far as to go against Josh? To go after him and get him fired?

"Oh my God." She let go of her handful of papers and they fluttered down around her.

"Oh my God, indeed." Apparently Ashley had let herself in. Wasn't she supposed to be having cocktails with Jill? "What the hell happened in here, babe?"

Heat flushed Elle's face as she surveyed the mess around her. Paper scattered like giant confetti across the hardwood floor. Ashley had walked in at just the right time to save her from tipping over the edge. Her eyes were thick with tears and she swallowed hard to fight them back. "I thought I could prove my mom didn't do it, but there's nothing here." She waved her hands at the chaos around her.

Ashley didn't seem to need any clarification on what "it" was. Her eyes softened with emotion, and she knelt next to Elle, wrapping her arms around her.

"Hey. It's okay," she murmured against Elle's neck. "It's okay. I'm here."

Ashley's touch did wonders for Elle. Her pounding heart shifted to a more regular beat and her breathing no longer came in desperate gulps. Her whole body felt more peaceful with the contact.

"I can't wrap my head around this," Elle said, rubbing her temples. A headache was setting in. Maybe she shouldn't have fought so hard to keep those tears from falling. "How could she do that to Josh? Or me? She had to know the shadow of what she did could haunt me when I was ready to return to acting. God, is that why everything in my career has felt like a fucking uphill battle since then? You know, I thought it was just the price for having a baby and taking time off when I did. I could live with that. But this? Did I even know my mother at all? I want to scream."

Ashley pulled back and raised an eyebrow. "So do it." She shrugged. "Go ahead and scream."

Elle took a deep breath and Ashley held hers as if bracing for a loud blast, but it just didn't feel right. This wasn't what she wanted or needed. "I don't want to scream. I want to scream *at her*." Hot tears of frustration burned her eyes again. It wasn't fair. "And I can't do that. I'll never have the chance to hear her explanation."

Ashley was silent while she played with Elle's hair, giving her the chance to compose herself. "You're right," she finally said. "You can't ask her, and that really sucks. It's a lot to process and you have to give yourself time for that. But the good news is, you're not alone. I am right here with you and I'm going to be by your side for whatever you need."

How the hell did she get so lucky? She took Ashley's hand, lacing their fingers, then leaned in to kiss her soft and soulful on her full, red lips. The mess of papers and noise in her head fell away and for the moment it was just the two of them and that kiss. Maybe everything wasn't okay, but maybe she could get through it as long as she had Ashley by her side.

She could never get her mother's side of the story, and Jill had no reason to lie. Her mother was always a strong-willed woman who knew how to get what she wanted, and her family was the absolute most important thing to her. Elle knew that much about her for certain. If Elle opened her mind and really thought about it, the stories kind of tracked.

She was going to have to face it—there was a damn good chance her mom really did have Josh written off the show. Tears slid slowly down her cheeks as reality set in. There was no way to change that now. No way to make it better for anyone.

CHAPTER NINETEEN

When the cast returned to the *Cook Off* kitchen set on Wednesday for the filming of Pasta Week, they were down to the last five contestants. As she tied her apron around her waist, Ashley surveyed her competitors. In addition to Elle and her there were the three guys: Benji, Michael, and of course, Mason. The mood was a lot more intense than before. It was as if everyone knew the competition had leveled up. There were only two more kitchen battles before the finals, and Ashley was ready to give it her best to get there.

She had originally planned on making pasta primavera, but fearing the judges would see the dish as too safe, she opted instead to go with a carbonara. Thank heavens she and Elle had made pasta from scratch three times on their time off from filming. Making the dough and using the pasta machine was becoming routine.

The more confident Elle had decided to go with a spinach and ricotta lasagna that included not only pasta made from scratch, but homemade béchamel and tomato sauces. She was such a shoo-in to win the whole thing, but Ashley would be a happy gal as long as she made it to the finals with her. The fact that she had made it as far as she had was amazing. Only three weeks earlier her cooking skills were limited to heating soup from a can and microwaving pizza rolls.

Ashley made a well with the dry ingredients on the countertop. She had just cracked the first egg when Freddie and a cameraman appeared at her workstation. It was her turn for an up-close-and-personal interview. She stood up straighter and arranged her expression into something she hoped conveyed cool and calm.

"Looks like we're making pasta by hand old-school style at Ashley Castle's station." Freddie waved the camera in closer to get the shot. "You've done this before, I can tell. Give us some insight on what's happening here."

Did he not just say what was happening there? But she knew the drill: smile, keep working, and give the director the soundbite he wanted.

"This is the way you make pasta from scratch." Ashley glanced up at the camera before focusing back on her work. "It's a simple recipe—flour, salt, olive oil, and eggs. I'm going to use a fork to slowly pull the dry ingredients into the eggs until I have a dough."

"All right. Sounds simple enough." Freddie nodded. "Is this a recipe you've perfected with your gal pal Elle Bissett?"

Ashley suddenly felt like her stomach was full of cement. Had someone found out her secret? That she only just learned how to cook and that Elle was the one teaching her? Did someone she'd trusted leak it? She and Elle had been careful at first, but lately they'd become sloppy—having Benji join them and Luci for meals, taking all that food to the woman's shelter. She remembered the way Nan had greeted her when they first met that day. "I recognized you the minute you pulled up." Or it could've been those damn Petersons. Had Janet decided to get revenge? After their disastrous lunch Ashley wouldn't put anything past her.

Oh my God, would they kick her off the show for cheating or something? Did they send Freddie over to her station to get a confession before a dramatic confrontation with Producer Kelly or the director? The camera was bearing down on her, waiting for the drama to erupt. After all the hard work she'd put in, she couldn't go down like that.

"Freddie, don't be silly." She hated the high-pitched giggle that accompanied her words. Where the hell was that coming from? She swiped at her forehead with the back of her wrist. "This is a traditional recipe. Practically everyone knows it, and if they don't know it, they could surely look it up on the Internet. It's not like it's some kind of Bissett family secret."

Freddie's pronounced eyebrows had pushed closer and closer as she rambled on until they'd finally met in the middle of his face like two kissing caterpillars. After an awkward on-camera silence, he finally reacted. "So the rumors *are* true— you've been spending time off set with your former teenage rival Elle Bissett?"

"What?" Ashley almost dropped her fork. So much for keeping their relationship under wraps. Her mind reeled for an appropriate response while the damn camera continued to stare at her, unwavering in its search for a juicy scoop. This was reality television. This was *her thing*. Time to rein it in. "Our teenage years are long behind us, but here in the *Cook Off* kitchen we've really bonded. All of us. We're all competitors, but we're friends too."

"Well, isn't that the sweetest?" Freddie spoke directly to the camera. "Friendship is the real prize here in the *Celebrity Cook Off* kitchen."

Ashley ignored the fact that Freddie was making a joke at her expense and gave the camera a sweet smile as it pulled back from her workstation. She turned her focus back to the task literally at hand—working her dough. Rolling and folding. Rolling and folding. The repetition was a little hypnotic and quite therapeutic. At least Freddie had moved on to Benji's station and the secret about her cooking lessons was safe.

As she worked the dough, the stress of the competition time-crunch and her botched interview eased out of her shoulders. By the time the task was completed she had shaken off her worry. Her dish was coming along, and she had a plan. The judges were going to love her creamy carbonara. With the dough needing to rest for an hour she finally felt like she could take a moment to breathe. She had nearly two hours left to finish the dish. No sweat.

She pulled out her recipe cards to review her next steps and check what she needed to grab from the community pantry, but she couldn't help checking out what her competition was up to. As surprised as she was to still be here, some of those still cooking were even more shocking in her estimation.

Michael always impressed the judges with his down-home cooking, so it seemed right that he was still around. But Mason and Benji—come on. Benji, as cute and charming as he was, was just a kid whose familiarity with cooking was mainly concocting weird things to eat for laughs on the Internet. Hardly gourmet cuisine.

And Mason Getty...ugh. She glanced at him as she meandered past his workstation on her way to the pantry. He was mugging for the camera, playing air drums with two wooden spoons, a box of pasta sitting on the counter beside him. When the filming started that day he had announced that he was making buffalo chicken and blue cheese mac. It sounded tasty, but boxed pasta in a pasta-dish competition? Seriously? It was a wonder he wasn't just whipping up a box of Kraft Dinner and calling it a day. How was he still in the competition at all?

Ashley's wandering thoughts came to a halt as she studied the community pantry. She would have to use pancetta as there was no guanciale. Elle had warned her she may need to make the substitution, so the revelation didn't throw her off her game. She would also need fresh basil, half-and-half to add the creamy element that gave her carbonara its name, eggs, and of course, a nice block of parmesan. It was a simple dish if you considered the elements. The art was in the making.

The clock ticked down while Ashley rolled the dough and cut the linguine, but she was still on schedule. As she was preparing to crisp the pancetta in the cast-iron skillet Elle had loaned her from her home, she glanced at the clock. There was just over an hour before the dishes were to be presented to the judges, and all around the kitchen the scramble was on.

Elle was looking chilled as ever as she slid her lasagna into the oven. For her the hard part was over. With a recipe that now just required an hour of baking, she would have smooth sailing until Freddie—the host with the most—called time was up. It was probably just a matter of minutes before Elle started up her social butterfly act like last time and made a tour of the kitchen.

Ashley exhaled deeply. That was not how the last hour of the competition was going to go for her. Her creamy carbonara sauce was going to need her full attention and she still had to attend to the linguine lingering on parchment-paper-lined trays waiting for its splashdown in the pot of boiling water. The timing of this dish was everything.

She focused on the oil heating in the skillet and tried to ignore the ruckus the guys were kicking up on the other side of the kitchen. Apparently, Mason had his macaroni and cheese into the oven and was trying to come up with some way to entertain himself while he waited for it to bake.

"Michael, think fast!" Mason called across the kitchen as he lobbed a loaf of Italian bread at the apron-clad athlete.

That's fine. Ashley didn't need to get distracted. Let them be jackasses. The cameras would eat it up. When push came to shove and dishes were presented to the judges, she would have her moment to shine. Add the pancetta to the skillet. That's a good sizzle. That's a *competition-winning* sizzle.

"Can you believe that dork?" Elle slid into Ashley's workspace once again. "Michael's still cooking. There should be a rule against distracting the other cooks."

Ashley shot her a look over her shoulder while she pushed the pancetta around the pan with a wooden spoon, but Elle didn't seem to notice. Elle was leaning back, elbows on the countertop, settled in. A little distracting in a totally different way. "I think tuning out the hullaballoo is part of the challenge."

"Hullaballoo," Elle repeated between nibbling chunks of parmesan she broke off the block. "That's a great word."

"It's not the kind of word you want around when you're trying to concentrate on getting something perfect though." The finish line was in sight. Ashley could push through. Keep her eyes on the prize, so to speak. "Ugh. I just want to serve my creamy carbonara to the judges, get through to the next round, and celebrate later tonight with you."

"I think that sounds like a fabulous plan and I have a few ideas of how we can celebrate." Elle waggled her eyebrows suggestively. "In fact—"

Shouts from across the kitchen interrupted her. "Just throw the bread!" Mason waved his arms above his head. "I'm wide open, you pussy!"

Elle pushed off the counter and stepped into the aisle separating the rows of workstations, hands on hips, a no-nonsense expression on her face. "Mason! Language! This is a family show!"

But her admonishment came too late. Michael had already released the loaf, and Mason with his eyes on the ball, did not see Elle had moved into the aisle. Ashley watched in horror as the next events seemed to unfold in slow motion.

The Italian bread hit Mason squarely in the chest, he caught it and did a little celebratory dance step backward. He plowed right into the startled Elle, who was thrown off-balance. She backpedaled and reached out to catch her balance on the countertop. Only instead of grabbing the counter, her arm pushed the sheets of resting linguine over the edge. And Ashley's homemade pasta crashed to the floor.

The blood rushed to Ashley's head and roared in her ears. For a moment the room spun around her. This could not be happening. To steady herself, she gripped the handle of the oven door like it was a handrail. The situation was embarrassing enough—she didn't need to pass out on camera too.

In a flash Elle was by her side, arm around her waist as if she could tell Ashley needed the extra support. "Ash, I'm so sorry. I didn't mean to…I was just trying to…" She squeezed her a little tighter and sighed. "Maybe they landed tray side down and they're fine?"

The shocked looks on the guys' faces didn't indicate she should hold on to hope, but Ashley leaned forward with Elle and peered over the counter nonetheless.

Tears stung the corners of her eyes as she surveyed the carnage. The pasta had not, in fact, landed tray side down. The strips of dough were scattered across the floor, dirty and ruined. Much like her chances of getting through to the next round of *Celebrity Cook Off.* There was no way to salvage her dish. She had nothing to serve the judges.

"My pasta's on the floor. It's on the floor." The most ridiculous phrase Ashley had ever uttered, but she could find no other words. Her brain slipped into autopilot. Maybe she was in shock. Her knees went weak and she collapsed onto the counter in defeat as her body felt the effect too.

"Ashley, I'm so sorry," Michael said, stepping over the mess on the floor to put a big, comforting hand on her shoulder. "We were just messing around. We should have been more careful."

"It will all be okay," Elle chimed in. Her voice sounded too gentle. Like if she didn't keep her tone happy-happy Ashley might completely shatter into a million little pieces. Kind of like the remains of her linguini on the floor below.

"How is this ever going to be okay? We're supposed to serve the judges a pasta dish and my pasta is…on the floor." Ashley sniffed. She had to pull herself together. She might get voted off the show, but she wouldn't cry on camera over spilled linguini. And those cameras were all starting to point in her direction as their operators became aware of the unfolding drama in her workstation. She needed a plan B. "I can't possibly make another batch. The dough has to rest for at least forty-five minutes and even that's pushing my luck to keep it from tearing when I handle it. I don't have that kind of time. What am I going to do?"

"Well, you could just use a box of spaghetti from the pantry." Mason shrugged. "Want me to grab you some?"

Her homemade creamy carbonara over pasta from a box? What was it with these men and their pasta from a box or bag? There was no way she was using that. Not after she spent all that time working on her recipe and how she'd learned to make pasta from scratch for this event. FROM SCRATCH. Ashley Castle, the woman who two weeks ago had to beg her employees to eat her cookies. No. No freaking way. She would not serve the judges pasta from a box. She'd come way too far for that. "No, Mason. No thank you."

"You can't serve sauce without—"

Elle cut Mason off. "Guys, we'll take it from here. Why don't you just give Ashley a little space? Go check on your own food or something."

Mason gave a little salute before moonwalking away, and before retreating Michael mouthed one last apology, his hands steepled together as if in prayer. When it was just the two of them, Ashley finally dared to meet Elle's gaze. Elle wouldn't make a big deal about her teary eyes. "Seriously, what am I going to do? I can't use the pantry pasta."

"No," Elle agreed and chewed her bottom lip. Thinking. Suddenly her face brightened. "Oh my God. I have left-over dough. I made more than I needed for my lasagna. It just needs to be rolled out and cut."

Typical Elle. Always making more food than was actually needed. Ashley remembered being astounded the first time she looked in her freezer at home.

"You're going to give me your dough?"

"It's left over. I've already used what I needed."

Ashley considered it. They used the same recipe, so what was the difference really? She didn't have time to start her own dough from square one, but she could swing rolling and cutting. "Is it legal for me to use your dough?"

"Legal?" Elle laughed.

"You know what I mean. Is it against the rules?" Ashley was surprised to find she was smiling despite the disaster at her workstation. It was because of Elle's laugh. She had that effect on her. Elle made everything better.

Elle shook her head. "I don't see why it would be against the rules. If you can use pasta from a box, why can't you use premade dough?"

Deciding Elle had a good point, Ashley accepted the donated dough and got back to work completing her dish.

"You've all brought us interesting pasta dishes." Freddie smiled his big, showbiz smile. The competitors were lined up in front of him like recruits being addressed by a drill sergeant.

A drill sergeant dressed in a flashy tailored jacket with crushed-velvet lapels. "But, as always, we have to say goodbye to one of you."

The judges' reveal segment was Ashley's least favorite part of the shoot every single time even when she knew her offering had been successful. It gave her a nervous stomach. Someone was getting kicked off the show and even if she didn't think it was going to be her, it still was uncomfortable.

"Let's start by letting everyone know who is safe this week," Freddie continued. "Elle, the judges loved your spinach and ricotta lasagna. You're safe. Benji, you served the judges spaghetti and meatballs. They called it a 'classic.' You're safe. And Ashley, your creamy carbonara was deemed a 'delight' by the judges. You are also safe. Unfortunately, that means Michael and Mason are the bottom two this week."

Michael and Mason took a reluctant step forward as instructed while everyone else took a cautionary step backward, widening the gap between them and *the bottom two*. Ashley was embarrassed by the wave of relief that washed over her. Whatever else happened, she had made it through to the next round. Elle reached over and gave her hand a quick squeeze. A quick telegraph that they would celebrate later.

Freddie clasped his hands in front of him and his features shifted into a more solemn expression. "Michael, the judges said your cheese ravioli in vodka cream sauce had zip, but your pasta was chewy, and they wanted more cheese. Mason, your buffalo chicken blue cheese mac showed creativity and the flavors worked well together, but they just couldn't get past your pasta from a box."

Mason groaned and Elle bumped her hip into Ashley's. Ashley had to bite the inside of her cheek to keep from laughing. Mason had played around for the entire episode and somehow expected to still slide by to the next round. His too-cool-for-school attitude had finally caught up with him.

A hush fell over the set and the cameras focused in on the two men awaiting their fate. Freddie seemed to relish a good dramatic pause. Finally, he broke the silence.

"I'm sorry, Mason. It's your time to leave the *Celebrity Cook Off* kitchen."

In every episode they had filmed up to that point those words had preceded hugs and goodbyes and a teary-eyed contestant exiting the set. Apparently, Mason was not going out like that.

"This is SO BOGUS!" He pulled his visor off his head and threw it to the ground. Freddie took a big step backward. Away from the wild-eyed, disgruntled contestant. This was not how things were supposed to go. "Totally fucking bogus."

"Take it easy, big guy," Elle muttered. "Family show, remember?"

Mason spun on his heel like he was doing one of his old boy-band dance moves. He growled as he zeroed in on Elle and Ashley. "Funny coming from you since you've been acting like this is some kind of freaking dating show."

"You got something to say to me?" Elle pushed up her sleeves and put her hands on her hips. Poised for battle. Totally ready to defend herself and Ashley.

"Oh yeah, I've got something to say to you *and* your girlfriend." Mason's face was twisted with ugly jealousy. "You're both fucking cheaters."

Kelly stomped onto the set. "What the hell is going on here?"

"This sucks is what's going on." Mason's face was tomato-sauce red. He swiped his hand through the sweat on his forehead. "So what if I used pasta from a fucking box? So what if I didn't make my own pasta? Neither did Ashley. At least I didn't cheat. There's no rule against boxed pasta, but I'm pretty sure someone helping you with your dish is totally against the rules."

"He's right." Kelly flipped through the pages on her clipboard as if searching for the exact wording. "Each contestant shall produce the dish on their own with no outside assistance. That's the rule on the books. Ashley, did someone else make part of your dish?"

Damn it. Ashley's legs felt like spaghetti. Was the ground beneath her actually shaking? And when had it become so hot in the studio? Had they turned the lights up brighter or something?

"I mean, yes Elle made the dough for my linguini, but that's only because of the accident in the kitchen. My handmade pasta was knocked onto the floor. I did all the work to roll and cut it into linguini. When she gave it to me, it was just a ball of dough."

"See? Cheating!" Mason exclaimed, his arms in the air in a victorious V.

It was true. She'd cheated. She'd used an element in her dish that someone else had made. When you said it like that, it *did* sound worse than Mason's pasta from a box. How would the *Queen of the Castle* fans react if she got the boot from the show because she cheated? Instead of boosting her homemaker cred this whole exercise would totally tank it. *God, what would the network think?*

"Accident my ass." Elle stepped between Ashley and Mason. Strong and protective. And not taking any shit from some overgrown boy bander. "Ashley's linguini was knocked on the floor because Mason was screwing around in the kitchen and distracting everyone with some macho bread-football shtick."

"Oh my God, get over yourself," Mason spat before turning to Kelly. "Come on, this is fucking ridiculous."

"Enough!" Kelly held her hands up in a call for order. "There's no rule against using ingredients from the pantry. There is, however, a rule against having someone else work on your dish. So, it's really simple. Ashley, did you have someone else work on your dish?"

"See, this is what's wrong with America," Elle interjected. "On that British baking show they encourage the contestants to be kind and help one another. It is peaceful and it is gentle. That's why people love it."

It was sweet of Elle to try to run interference for her, but Ashley had to own up to her actions. She didn't mean to cheat, but she had. She'd used Elle's dough to make her linguini. She broke the rules and she had to speak up.

She put a reassuring hand on Elle's shoulder as she stepped around her. "I did, Kelly. My pasta was made from the dough Elle made."

Kelly's eyes were full of disappointment when she met Ashley's gaze. "Then I'm sorry, but my hands are tied here. Mason, you get a pass this week. Ashley, it's time for you to leave the *Celebrity Cook Off* kitchen. Guys, let's call it a wrap. We'll sort this out in edits."

Kelly had already turned and started walking off set when Elle called after her, "Wait! It was my idea for Ashley to use the dough. I'm the one who cheated and I'm the one who should leave the show."

"What?" Ashley spun to face Elle. She couldn't let her do this. It wasn't any more Elle's fault than her own. And, yes, she needed the screen time on the show, but Elle did too. "No. It was my dish that was ruined and I'm the one responsible for what I presented to the judges. It's okay. I'll leave the show."

"But it wasn't your fault your dish was ruined," Elle argued. Her big brown eyes, full of tenderness, searched Ashley's face. "Hell, I'm the one who knocked your pasta off the table. I'm the one who should leave."

"Look, I don't care which one of you leaves." Kelly had clearly run out of patience with this situation. She probably had other decisions to make, other shows to plan, other shit to take care of. "But one of you is out. Everyone else, be back on set Friday morning to shoot Dessert Week."

"Okay, see you Friday," Freddie said with his big host wolf grin as if the whole dough-gate cheating scandal didn't just completely blow up.

Michael and Mason made hasty exits as well, as if hanging around still put them at risk of being booted off the show. Benji glanced at Elle and Ashley sympathetically, but ultimately gave a sheepish wave and left the set too.

Finally, it was just the two of them, Ashley and Elle, on the empty soundstage staring at each other.

Ashley took Elle's hand and intertwined their fingers. She knew Elle had made up her mind, and she'd learned enough in the past couple of weeks with this beautiful woman to know that was that. There was no turning back once Elle had set her mind on what she wanted. She was so stubborn, and insistent, and absolutely loyal and loving. "I don't want you to do this."

"I know you don't. But I'm doing it."

"Then I'll quit too." Ashley couldn't just sit by and let Elle do this. She deserved to go to the next round as much as anyone.

Elle frowned. "No. Don't do that. If you quit too then there was no point in me quitting. I meant it when I said you earned your spot here. You've worked so hard. I want to see what you do with it. I really, really want this for you. So, it's settled. You're staying and I'm out. Beat them all and win this thing."

"Elle, I—"

"And speaking of out," Elle continued without waiting for further protest, "I've gotta run."

"Run where? What about our…" Damn. Celebration wasn't the right word anymore. The day had totally tanked. And as rough as it had been on Ashley, Elle was the one out of a job. "Do you want to come over later?"

Suddenly it was like Elle couldn't get out the door fast enough. "I'll text you."

CHAPTER TWENTY

Elle sat in her El Camino and tried to wrap her mind around what the hell just happened. She had served the best pasta dish by far to those judges and yet here she was, ejected from the show.

All she knew was when Mason started coming for Ashley she had to step in and protect her. And she couldn't let Ashley take the blame for breaking the rules. It had been Elle's idea to share the dough in the first place. She had to speak up. It was instinct. It was right.

Now she was out of a job.

She didn't regret what she'd done. Well, not the leaving-so-Ashley-could-stay part anyway. But that didn't mean she wasn't going to need some time to process the consequences of her actions. First she got the appalling and disturbing news about her mother getting Josh fired, and now this. It was…a lot.

She'd pulled into her driveway over ten minutes ago and had been sitting there since. Dragging her feet was not making the haze that had settled in her brain go away. It was time to go in the house. Baby steps.

She hadn't even closed the door behind her when Luci came bounding down the hall from the kitchen and wrapped her mom in a bear hug.

"Mom! Mom, I can't believe you did that! Giving up your spot on the show for Ashley. I mean, it's so romantic. But still. I can't believe you did it. You love cooking and you totally could've won the whole competition. Are you okay, Mom?"

Oh, to have the enthusiasm and energy of a teenage girl.

"Sweetie, I'm fine. I didn't give up my spot for Ashley. I made a mistake that got us both in trouble. One of us had to go." She kissed the top of her daughter's head. "And how did you find out so fast?"

Luci released her from the mega-hug. "Benji called me as soon as he left the studio." She shrugged. "But I would've known something was wrong anyway when Aunt Mari showed up with stuff to make margaritas."

"Marigold's here?" Uh-oh. Elle had some explaining to do.

On cue Marigold entered the living room carrying a pitcher of margaritas and two glasses.

"Cocktails anyone?" Marigold set the glasses on the coffee table and began to pour. "Luci, run into the kitchen for me and grab the tray of chips and salsa. There's a Mountain Dew in the fridge for you too."

"She doesn't need that kind of caffeine. Have you seen her energy level?" Elle collapsed onto the sofa as she called after Luci who was already on her way to the fridge. "You don't need caffeine!"

"Give her a break, we're celebrating here." Marigold held up her drink in a salute and took a sip.

"Celebrating? Aren't you pissed at me? The whole drive home I worked on the perfect speech to explain to you what happened today and now here you are at my house where I wasn't expecting you. And you don't even have the decency to be pissed?"

"Pissed?" Marigold blinked her fake eyelashes dramatically. So very Marigold. "Because you begged me to get you this gig and I pulled a bunch of strings and worked my special brand of magic, and then you threw it all away to play hero in front of your girlfriend?"

"See? That was exactly the kind of conclusion I was afraid you would jump to." Elle shook her head. She knew Marigold would forgive her. Eventually. They'd been through too much together. A lost gig wasn't going to be the end of them. But she at least owed her best friend an explanation. "It actually wasn't like that at all."

"Really?" Marigold scooted over on the couch to make room for Luci who had returned with the snacks. And that damn Mountain Dew. "So tell me what it was like."

"Well, it was more like…" Elle nibbled at a chip while she attempted to reframe the day's events in a way that wasn't going to sound exactly as Marigold had put it. She came up empty. "No, you're right. That's pretty much what happened. Go ahead. Be pissed."

"I'm not going to do that," Marigold said. She licked some salt from the rim of her glass. She had really gone all out with those margaritas. She was remarkably calm for someone who was pissed off. Maybe she really wasn't. "Darling, we have been best friends since we were kids. I'm choosing not to be pissed about this."

"And that's why we're celebrating." Elle punctuated her summary with a crunch of corn chip.

"We're celebrating because now you're free for the next project."

Elle nearly did a spit take with her margarita. Marigold was always good for putting a positive spin on a not-so-great situation, but had she actually said those glorious words? "Oh my God! You've found me another project already? You are amazing, Mari."

"I am amazing, just not *that* amazing." Marigold smirked her glass-is-half-full kind of expression. "I don't have another project for you. Yet. But something will come, Elle. *Celebrity Cook Off* will give you four weeks of great exposure when it airs. You've done what you set out to do and it will pay off. Just be patient. You don't need the money, so you don't have to worry about that. Try to hang out and relax and wait for the next big thing to come along. I'm your agent, so listen to me. It's going to be okay."

"Okay." Elle took a long drink of margarita and waited for the tequila to work its magic. Marigold just said it was going to be okay, and she was probably right. *Cook Off* really had been a good way to get her face on television and her name out there again. Surely she would reap the benefits in the very near future. Another gig would come along just like Mari said.

"There is one other thing we need to talk about."

There it was. The margaritas weren't celebratory—they were conciliatory. She took another fortifying gulp. *Come on, tequila.* "Okay, Mari. Hit me."

Marigold sighed and pulled a rolled-up gossip rag out from the messenger bag on the floor beside her. She'd clearly planned ahead for the moment. This couldn't be good. "I'm sorry, Elle. I don't know how this story got out."

Elle held her breath as she scanned the page. The picture was an old publicity shot of the cast from *Sugar and Spice*, but it was the headline that made her mouth go dry.

THE REAL STORY BEHIND THE END OF TELEVISION'S SUGAR AND SPICE

Fifteen Years Later the Truth About Josh Peterson's Hasty Departure From the Show Revealed

"Oh no," Elle managed. "They didn't. They wouldn't…"

"I don't know how the story leaked." Marigold shook her head sadly. "It wasn't me, I can promise you that."

"No, I know." It was crystal clear to Elle how it happened. Nobody in that town had given a second thought to Josh in the past fifteen years until they started shooting *Celebrity Cook Off* and the producers had those damn paparazzi follow all the contestants around looking for any scrap of dirt that could be exploited to give the show visibility. They would apparently do anything to get the general public talking about the competitors, even to the detriment of the competitors. Drum up a little buzz for the show no matter what it took. In their minds, any publicity was good publicity, but in Elle's mind, not so much.

"God, it was the fucking paparazzi the producers have tailing us constantly. Damn it. My mother kept this secret buried for years and now that she's gone it's going to blow up in my face. It's just as well I got the boot from *Cook Off*. Nobody is going to work with me after this anyway. I'd probably be the scourge of the kitchen. I'll be poisonous. Oh my God, I hope I don't infect Ashley's career too."

"Elle." Marigold put a comforting hand on her knee. "Hey. One step at a time here, okay? Let's focus on the things we can control. You happen to have some time on your hands, and we need to give you some good press, so I'm going to give Nan a call and see if we can't set up a time to bring some food to the shelter and maybe get someone to do a little happy news story on it. We'll start there."

Perhaps Marigold was right, and a little counter-press would do the trick. "Okay. We'll start there." Elle didn't see any choice but to agree as she took another hearty swallow of margarita. That tequila magic could kick in any time now.

After the impromptu fiesta ended, Marigold left, and Elle cleaned up the kitchen. Her body was on autopilot. Same old task, different day. That's how it would be until she found her next gig. She may as well get used to it.

She poured herself a big glass of iced tea and went out to sit in the backyard. The late afternoon sun was bright but felt like heaven on her face. It was probably wreaking havoc on her skin, the sweet heat ushering in fine lines and wrinkles. Her mother would really be giving her hell right about now for not putting on one of those big, floppy hats before coming outside to bask in the sun.

Her gaze settled on the crepe myrtle her mother had planted in the far corner of the yard. Who was she kidding? Hélène Bissett would be giving her hell for a lot more than not wearing a hat. If she knew what Elle had done in the studio earlier, she would bring new meaning to the phrase *freak the fuck out*. Of course, Elle would have a few choice words for her mom too. Her stomach dropped every time she thought about that damn gossip-rag story. What a fucking mess.

Dammit, Mom. How could she have gone to the producers like that?

Maybe Marigold and the *Cook Off* contestants thought Elle was trying to be some kind of hero on the set, but she knew the damn truth. She couldn't get another coworker fired for something for which she was equally responsible. Not after the way things had spiraled last time.

She liked Ashley. Really liked her. But what if this story about *Sugar and Spice* really did make Elle into a pariah and she became toxic to everyone associated with her? Like Ashley. Elle couldn't get the idea out of her head that disaster was sure to follow any time she became involved with another actor. God knew that was one of the ideas her mom had planted in her mind just like she'd planted the crepe myrtle. She'd watered, fed and tended the idea until it put down roots. Now all these years later, manufactured or not, Elle's fear was still in full bloom. She wanted to be with Ashley, but maybe it was best for them to break things off now before both their careers totally blew up.

That was why she had sent that ridiculous text in response to the multiple inquiries Ashley had made about her well-being.

I'm fine. I just need some time alone. Talk later.

She needed some time to sulk, but not about leaving *Celebrity Cook Off*. She was sulking while considering breaking up with a woman she…really liked. She just couldn't drag Ashley's career down with hers. She cared about her too much.

CHAPTER TWENTY-ONE

"The steak smells amazing," Jill said as she filled the water glasses. "What else can I do to help?"

It was Sunday evening, the night before the *Cook Off* finale, and Ashley was a bundle of nerves. The table on the shaded back patio was already set beautifully and dinner was sizzling away on the grill, but Ashley was grateful for her agent's presence. "The potato salad is in a turquoise bowl in the fridge." She nodded toward the French doors that led into the kitchen. She made a special "loaded bacon ranch" version of the summer meal classic that Benji had found on the Internet and shared with her, and she couldn't wait to see how it was received. "Would you grab a serving spoon for it too, please?"

After acing Dessert Week on *Celebrity Cook Off* Friday with her cannoli, Ashley had gone straight to work creating her menu for the upcoming final: Grill Week. She'd decided on grilled flank steak, grilled broccoli, and the potato salad. She would cap it off with grilled watermelon for dessert.

With Elle off the grid and working through her own issues, Ashley had had to come up with her own menu. She took Benji's advice and turned to YouTube to bone up on grilling skills, but when it came down to it, the kitchen basics Elle had drilled into her head carried her through. Now all that was left to do was test her results out on Jill. And, of course, manage to re-create the meal in the competition the next morning.

She turned the steak just as Jill rejoined her outside. "Seriously, Ash, I can't get over how far you've come with your cooking."

"Well, I really appreciate you coming over to be my guinea pig." Ashley meant it, but she couldn't stop the sigh that slipped out. There was no denying the past few days had been rough on her. She pulled the broccoli florets from the grill and arranged them neatly on a small platter. "It's been pretty quiet around here lately."

Jill's face was full of sympathy. "Still no word from Elle?"

Ashley hadn't actually talked to Elle since they'd left the studio Wednesday. Once Elle actually picked up when Ashley called her, but after quickly assuring her she was fine, she'd made a feeble excuse to go and clicked off. They'd texted a little. Barely. But that was it. Four days of near silence. She was trying to give Elle the time she needed to process what happened on set, but the lack of communication was wearing on her. She was grateful to Jill for agreeing to Sunday dinner not just for a taste test, but also to talk to *someone*.

"Not really. I'm giving her the space she needs."

"Hmmm." Jill literally seemed to be biting her tongue.

"I know that 'hmmm.' You have an opinion." Ashley carried the steak and broccoli to the table and the women sat. "You may as well tell me what it is."

Jill shrugged. "It's just weird. Elle always struck me as so straightforward. I wouldn't think she'd react this way to getting kicked off a reality TV show."

Sadness tugged at Ashley's heart. In some ways the *Cook Off* experience had gone so much better than she'd expected. No one who really knew her would have ever guessed she'd end up in the final, and yet there she was. But when it came to Elle Bissett, her head was spinning, and as much as she hated to admit it, things were not going the way she'd planned. "You know, I really thought it would be the two of us going into that final. Thank God that creep Mason got the boot Friday. I couldn't stand it if he had one of the final slots instead of Elle. Anyway, I know she wanted to be there too, and she sacrificed her spot for me which was incredibly sweet. So she's processing everything, I guess. I can be patient."

"And she's dealing with what she just learned about her mother. I saw the tabloid story. That had to hurt."

Ashley nodded. She'd had that very same concern, but it wasn't the kind of thing you wanted to address via a text. She wanted to be there for Elle, but it was damn hard to do that if Elle wasn't going to let her in. "I'm sure you're right. And I'll be here when she's ready to talk it all through, but apparently today is not that day. I'm not going to give up on her though. She'll talk about it when she's ready."

"You should continue to be patient then. She'll come around eventually," Jill said between bites. She nodded enthusiastically and at first Ashley thought that was a comment on her relationship strategy, but it quickly became clear that the reaction was more about the food. They were on to the next topic. "I've never had broccoli grilled before. This is delicious."

"Thank you. It's so simple—oil, lemon juice, garlic salt—and voilà." Ashley had never had it before either, but she suspected the side dish could become a go-to recipe in her kitchen. Thank you, YouTube.

She was not quite as confident in the way she was handling things with Elle, and it was still tickling at the corners of her mind, despite Jill's attempt to change the subject. "You really think I'm doing the right thing? With Elle, I mean. Do you think I'm doing the right thing with Elle?"

"Giving her space? Yes. For now anyway. Get through tomorrow's finale and then you can sort out your love life. Keep your focus on your work for one more day. You need this, and you said Elle wants it for you. You should honor that by doing your best in the competition tomorrow. Everything else will wait."

"I can do that," Ashley agreed, but she wasn't exactly sure how easy it would be. One more day of putting her feelings for

Elle on hold and trying to not worry about her. Jill had been right when she said this wasn't like Elle, usually so confident no matter what she did. "Wait, didn't you say you had news for me?"

When they spoke on the phone earlier, Jill had mentioned that she had something good to share with her, and more than once as she prepared for their dinner Ashley's mind had wandered to what it could be. She'd hoped it would be something about Elle, maybe that it had been confirmed she would be in the studio for the *Cook Off* final in the stands with the others eliminated from the competition. But clearly Jill had no inside information regarding the subject of Elle Bissett. Maybe it was something else related to the competition like a promotional spot on a talk show. It would be fun if a few of the contestants got to do press together before the show aired. God, that would've been a lot of fun to do with Elle as a finalist too. Anyway, she was ready to hear Jill's news. The perfect distraction.

"Oh, darling." Jill took a long drink of water, building the drama. "I heard from the network this morning. It seems the *Celebrity Cook Off* producers have leaked just enough bits and pieces teasing the show to create some good buzz, and fans of *Queen of the Castle* are eating it up."

Leaked bits and pieces sounded somewhat dubious, but fans were always a positive. "What are you saying?"

"I'm saying they're renewing *Queen of the Castle* for another season. Congratulations!"

"They're...renewing *Queen of the Castle*?" The words didn't make sense to her. Like they were in a language she'd studied back in high school but didn't keep up with. She shook her head to try to clear it. With her focus on learning to cook and surviving in the competition, not to mention her fledgling relationship—or whatever it was—with Elle, she'd somehow managed to push all thoughts of *Queen of the Castle* to the very back of her mind. Funny how it used to be the only thing she could think about and now...

"Ashley." Jill quirked a perfectly plucked eyebrow expectantly. "Did you hear me? They're renewing your show. You got what you wanted. You did it."

All her hard work, the cooking lessons, the hours of practicing and perfecting recipes. It had paid off. She'd done what she needed to do—she saved her show. Like Jill said, it was what she'd wanted. And yet...

She was glad the show had been renewed. She was more than appreciative of the steady work. But she was also kind of digging the idea of working on that book with Elle. Fact was, as much as she loved David as a person, she didn't want to be the star of a show about her life as the woman who broke up with David Carlson. She was a lot more than that woman now and it turned out she didn't need the security blanket that *Queen of the Castle* had become for her. She wanted to be the star of a show about Ashley Castle. And that was going to require some changes if she was going to continue with another season.

Jill was still staring at her, but her previously amused expression was clouding with concern. Obviously she expected Ashley to react differently.

"Oh, yes." Ashley fixed a smile on her face. Time to take control of her life. "That's wonderful news. I...I think I have some champagne in the fridge. We should celebrate! And maybe talk about some plans for the next season. I have a few ideas."

CHAPTER TWENTY-TWO

"She works hard for the money!" Elle belted out the lyrics along to the music on the Movie Hits channel using her spoon as a microphone. "So hard for it, honey."

"Mom. Mom! You're making the song sound sad." Luci's disapproving look and whiny voice was accompanied by a hearty helping of pity. Like she was eyeing up a mom who sounded *and* looked sad.

"I'm sorry, honey." Elle pushed the O-shaped noodles in her bowl around. The spoon back to its regular duty. "Pass me that shaky cheese, please."

Just as Elle sprinkled the processed parmesan from the green plastic shaker, Marigold walked through the door, arms around a bag full of groceries. Based on the way her jaw dropped two steps in, she was not impressed by what she saw. Elle had the distinct feeling that she was in trouble.

Marigold set the brown-paper sack on the kitchen counter and blew out a long breath. "Okay." She drew the word out, possibly summoning patience. "Looks like I showed up just in the nick of time. What's going on here?"

"We're eating pasta from a can." Elle forced cheerfulness. It certainly wasn't inspired by the dinner of spaghetti hoops.

"I see." Marigold opened the fridge and inspected the contents. Since she hadn't been to the market in days, Elle could've told her there was nothing much to see in there. Her brow furrowed. "Where did you even get pasta from a can?"

"Benji brought it over." Luci grinned. "We ran out of Mom's frozen leftovers yesterday."

Luci didn't seem to mind the spaghetti hoops. In cartoon-font bubble letters, the can said that a serving contained a whole serving of vegetables. They couldn't be all *that bad*, although they didn't taste all that good either.

"That was gentlemanly of Benji." Marigold smiled at Luci before she frowned in Elle's direction. "No more frozen leftovers, eh? Sounds serious."

"It is serious." Elle dropped her spoon in the bowl and pushed it away. Marigold's gaze moved on to survey the sink full of dirty dishes. Another housekeeping fail. "I've lost the will to cook."

"And to clean too," Marigold deadpanned. "Dirty dishes, an entrée from a can, and don't think I missed that Mountain Dew in the fridge. Something is very, very wrong. Are you drunk?"

"She's not drunk. And Benji brought me the Mountain Dew," Luci volunteered. She was such a good kid. "Mom's just sad because she hasn't talked to Ashley in four days. But she's too stubborn to pick up the phone and tell Ashley she misses her."

"Smart kid." Marigold finally ended her critique of the kitchen and sat down at the table. "Lu, why don't you go play some Xbox and let Aunt Mari have a little chat with your mom?"

"Say no more." Luci raised her hands in surrender as she stood. "You're talking about yourself in the third person. I'm out."

As Luci shuffled out of the kitchen, Elle propped her feet up on the chair across from Mari and settled in for the lecture she suspected was coming from her best friend. "All right. Let me have it."

Marigold rubbed at her temples and pressed her lips together in one tight, bright-red line as if searching for some inner peace. "I'm worried about you. What's really going on?"

"What's going on is by avoiding Ashley I'm avoiding tanking her career too. And all that avoiding is crushing me. But I can see the writing on the wall: I'm going to ruin yet another costar's career simply by sleeping with them."

"You are not going to tank Ashley's career just by association, and that's not exactly what happened with Josh either." Marigold scrunched up her nose. Her thinking face. "Why won't you just talk to Ashley? You obviously miss her."

Elle felt the muscles in her jaw tighten. "If I talk to her I'm going to have to break up with her, and I really don't want to."

"There is absolutely no reason you have to break up with this woman." Marigold was speaking slowly, like she thought that might aid in understanding. "Although, the way you've treated her the past four days, she may want to break up with you."

There was Elle's other fear. That she was so messed up that she sabotaged the one good romantic relationship she'd had in…well, forever. She couldn't blame Ashley one bit if she was angry about the way she'd behaved the past few days. Elle had ignored most of her calls altogether and Ashley's texts to which she did respond were mostly short one-word replies. Which was worse, purposefully pushing people away or not being able to resist doing so? It didn't matter. Either way she'd fucked up big time.

"I can't stand the thought of ruining Ashley's career because she's sleeping with me and we're…dating or whatever. Hell, Josh only slept with me once and look what happened to him."

"Oh, Eleanor." Marigold reached across the table to take Elle's hand. Her emerald eyes shimmered with sympathy. "This is not the same thing as that at all, sweetie. You're not the victim of a curse or something. Josh was a man, and you were a child. He knew the potential consequences of his actions. He was the only one to blame for losing his job on *Sugar And Spice*, whether your mom went to the producers or not. He's lucky he didn't go to jail."

"I willingly had sex with him. I knew what I was doing too. My career stalled out, but my life went on. He ended up dead."

"He overdosed. That's not your fault either. Or your mother's. He'd had a substance use disorder for years. Long before he knew you."

Elle could feel the lump building in her throat. Mari just didn't get it. "He found out I was pregnant with his baby, he got kicked off the show because of my mom, and then he overdosed. I can plainly see a connection in that chain of events." The tears finally spilled over.

"I'm not saying it wasn't tragic. It was." Marigold squeezed Elle's hand tighter, keeping her tethered to the conversation. "What I'm saying is none of these things were your fault, and you need to stop blaming yourself. Josh lost his battle with addiction, but everything you listed in that chain of events before that was the result of action he took."

"That's not true. He wouldn't have lost his job if my mother hadn't gone to the producers and told them it was his baby," Elle whispered. "And if he hadn't lost his job, then maybe…"

"You had no control over her doing that. You didn't even know she had done it until now. I know it might be hard to see it this way, but I believe she was only protecting her daughter. She did what she thought was right. She couldn't have known what Josh was going to do next, or that he would end up overdosing. Her only thoughts were to protect you from getting involved with an adult man when you were still a minor." Marigold scooted her chair closer until she could reach to take Elle in her arms, letting her cry while she held her. "Elle, Josh Peterson didn't die because he had sex with you or because your mother told the producers of the show. He lost his battle with addiction."

"But he didn't—"

"No." Marigold's voice was firm, but still held warmth. "You need to stop second-guessing the past. I know you and Josh weren't in love, you were just experimenting sexually. I remember. But you were friends, and I don't for one second believe that he would want you punished for what happened, so please, sweetie, stop punishing yourself. You're happy with

Ashley and she seems happy with you. Don't let the paparazzi, or the Petersons, or anyone else for that matter decide what's best for the two of you."

Elle breathed deeply to get her tears under control. She wanted to be with Ashley, and only the two of them could decide if being together was right. She at least owed Ashley the chance to make up her mind for herself.

"I think you might be right, Mari."

"Of course I'm right. I'm your agent." Marigold kissed her on the top of her head. "Now what do you say we toss the spaghetti hoops and make some Niçoise salad. I happen to have all the ingredients in that bag on the counter."

"Even anchovies?"

"Except for anchovies."

CHAPTER TWENTY-THREE

Two hours to cook a complete grilled dinner sounded like ample time until you got to the nitty-gritty elements—marinading a flank steak and boiling potatoes for the salad. Ashley was thirty minutes into the competition before she had a moment to breathe much less worry about all the former contestants who had returned to watch from the stands built on set especially for the occasion. The whole gang was there, from Carina LaTraine, the soap star who was the very first to leave the *Cook Off* kitchen, to the very last to go—freaking Mason Getty. And sitting right there in the middle of all of them was Elle.

Ashley hadn't heard anything back after that last text to Elle the night before, which only reinforced what Jill had said. Ashley needed to focus on the competition for one more day and deal with her relationship after the show was over. That was especially true now when she had under ninety minutes to produce an award-winning meal. She had bacon to crisp and broccoli to chop. Plenty of other things to do besides obsess over whether or not Elle was cheering her on in the stands.

She lit the stovetop flame under her bacon-filled cast-iron skillet, bringing it up to temperature along with the pan, just like Elle had taught her, and drained the potatoes to cool. Task by task was the way to get through the competition.

A glance in the direction of Benji's workstation confirmed the teenager had his hands just as full as she did. He was multitasking—skewering seasoned brussels sprouts while boiling sweet potatoes to grill as a side dish to his bleu cheeseburgers. The sweet and buttery aroma of his caramelizing onions had been wafting over and invading her air space for a while, reminding Ashley of that day in Elle's kitchen making quiche. The day of their almost-first kiss.

A pop and sizzle from her own stovetop brought her attention back to her bacon. She should know better than to turn her back on her dish; she didn't need another kitchen mishap like she'd had during Pasta Week. She grabbed some metal tongs and pushed the strips in the pan, shifting them slightly to make sure they weren't sticking and burning.

Was Elle also remembering that day they crisped bacon and cooked onions in the grease left behind? The day they started whatever they'd been doing until five days ago when Elle shut it down and went radio silent. Ashley sighed and turned the bacon. She had to stop thinking about Elle. She had a competition to win.

Thirty minutes later, Ashley was in the homestretch. The loaded potato salad was assembled, the broccoli seasoned, and she was ready to fire up the grill. She ran back to the common pantry to grab some chives to garnish her potato salad.

"Trying to spice things up here at the end of the fourth quarter?" Michael teased, reaching his long arm around her to grab a basket of strawberries.

"I am so close to victory, I can taste it." She'd spent enough time in the kitchen with him by now to know how to give it right back. Yet another thing Elle had taught her to do. "Just need a little topper for my loaded bacon ranch potato salad."

Michael's jaw dropped and he bobbled his berries. "You're serving the judges loaded bacon ranch potato salad? With bacon and chives?"

Oh no, no no. "And shredded cheddar?"

He nodded slowly. "Sounds like we both had the same inspiration."

"Benji and his Internet find?" she asked.

"Benji and his Internet find," Michael confirmed. "The kid played us good."

"That little brat!" Ashley laughed and pressed a palm to her forehead. Part of her wanted to be angry at the teen for tricking them, but another part of her figured when it came to the competition, all was fair in love and cooking. Everyone wanted to be the last person standing. It was basically survival of the fittest. Besides, she could have done better reconnaissance if she was that concerned about duplicate dishes. She'd asked the guys what they were grilling, but not their sides. The only reason she'd known about Benji's sweet potatoes and sprouts was because his workstation was directly in front of hers and she'd seen it.

"What are we gonna do?" Michael lowered his voice. Recognizing drama brewing, the cameras were zooming in on their conversation.

"We're going to serve the same side dish." She shrugged. There was just over thirty minutes until they had to present their dinners. They would serve the same recipe. It was a crap break, but it wasn't the end of the world. "I don't know what else we can do."

"Okay," Michael agreed. "May the best loaded potato salad win, I guess."

"Yeah...right." Ashley didn't like the thought of putting up the same side as a competitor, but she couldn't very well tell Michael what he could or couldn't serve. She grabbed a bundle of chives and rushed back to her worktop.

She checked the heat on her grill. It was almost time to start her steak, but she just couldn't get over the side dish thing. What could she possibly throw together in the next thirty minutes that would be hearty enough to pair with steak and complex enough to impress the judges? She could roast some corn on the cob, but she'd still have to do something to push it to the next level. All she had to do was figure out what the hell that something was. The circling television cameras that seemed to sense her dilemma weren't helping her think.

Come on. Push it to the next level.

Great. Although she hadn't been around her for almost a week, Elle's words were still there etched in her brain as if she'd just heard them. She glanced over at the stands and saw Elle, twirling a pen between her fingers just like she'd done with the pencil the day they'd refinished her kitchen table. Ugh. Sure, just when she was starting to feel annoyed by Elle giving her the silent treatment, Elle had to go looking all adorable and reminding Ashley of all her sweet parts.

Had it really been three weeks since they'd gone to the farmers' market together and Elle had given her advice about making simple ingredients into something special? Elle had talked about roasting corn on the grill that day—how she cut it off the cob and added it to a simple salad and push it to the next level.

That was it! Ashley dashed back to the common pantry to grab a couple of ears of corn to throw on the grill. While her steak cooked she could mix up an easy honey balsamic dressing. She could make a fresh, chunky salad that would pair perfectly with red meat.

Elle might be mad or sad, or whatever her unspoken emotion, but she'd saved the day yet again.

Freddie Simon stood before the three remaining contestants, hands in his suit pockets, looking casual and cool despite having their fates on the tip of his tongue. Ashley shifted her weight and clenched her jaw, bracing herself.

"Benji, the judges called your bleu cheeseburger, 'heaven on a bun,' but your roasted sweet potatoes were burned and 'charcoal-like,'" he said, disappointment clouding his features. "Ashley, your flank steak was 'life changing' according to the judges and they loved the originality of your grilled broccoli. But they couldn't help but notice the last-minute changeup to your menu."

Would they really hold that against her? All the judges seemed to enjoy her fire-roasted corn, tomato, and avocado salad. Was there some kind of rule against switching your menu mid-episode now? She swallowed hard and forced herself to keep smiling as she nodded acknowledgment of Freddie's assessment of her performance. The cameras were no doubt studying her intently.

"And, Michael," Freddie continued. "Your barbeque chicken knocked the judges' socks off, but they called your potato salad, 'pedestrian.'"

Michael cringed and Ashley blew out a breath of relief. That could've been her pedestrian potato salad the judges were disparaging. Benji hadn't sabotaged her with that Internet-recipe stunt—he'd actually saved her butt.

"Only one of you can be the *Celebrity Cook Off* Champion." He paused, his expression smug. For one brief, shining moment he knew all the answers and held all the power. It was obvious he was hooked on the feeling.

To her left, Benji was rocking on his heels. On her right, Michael was standing with his back ramrod straight, his expression stoic, like he had shut out everything around him. They said good athletes were able to do that. Ashley's smile was so forced the muscles in her cheeks were starting to shake and thanks to the bright studio lights, she felt a sweat rising on her forehead. Couldn't this guy just spit it out already?

"That champion is," Freddie said, spreading his arms wide to emphasize the magnitude of his next words, "Ashley Castle. You're our *Celebrity Cook Off* winner!"

Elle was the first one on her feet, pumping her fist in the air and unleashing a loud, "Whoop!" Then the studio broke out in applause and cheers. Freddie turned to the camera and filmed his closing statements to sign off. Michael pulled Ashley into a congratulatory bear hug and Benji piled on. Ashley's heart was pounding in her ears and tears of happiness spilled over.

She'd actually done it. She'd gone from someone who faked the cooking segments on *Queen of the Castle* and could barely microwave popcorn without setting off the smoke detectors in her kitchen, to the winner of a nationally televised cooking competition. And she never could have done it without Elle.

The guys finally released their hold on Ashley and she threw her hands into the air in victory. She turned to the stands to yell over to Elle. The other former competitors were cheering and waving to her, even Mason, but the one person she wanted to celebrate with wasn't there.

Elle had gone.

CHAPTER TWENTY-FOUR

Elle sat on the lush, green grass, pinching the blades between her fingers. After she'd left the television studio, she'd driven around aimlessly—or so she thought—but she wasn't totally surprised when she ended up at Legacy Lawn Cemetery where her mother was buried.

She'd been absolutely thrilled for Ashley. All the hard work, the hours they spent practicing in the kitchen—it had all paid off. And as much as Elle had wanted to be participating in the finals herself, when Freddie called Ash's name, Elle thought her heart would burst with pride. Ashley had started out with something to prove and ended up going the distance. It was a hell of an accomplishment. Ashley was a hell of a woman.

That was why Elle had made her quick escape from the studio while everyone else was cheering. Ashley Castle deserved someone who wouldn't just stop communicating with her for days on end because she'd freaked out. Ashley deserved someone who was capable of having a real, adult relationship. She deserved someone who wasn't Elle.

"Damn it, Ma. You know this is all your fault," she said, squinting against the dappled sunshine filtering through the trees. She stared at the headstone as if expecting a response. That was stupid. It wasn't her mother. Her mother's body was in that location, her mother wasn't. But Elle had things she had to say. Sitting there with the warm earth beneath her and the peaceful quiet of the open air it seemed like maybe her mom could hear her. "I trusted you. I believed everything you said, and now after all these years I find out you were keeping this huge secret from me. You were the one who got Josh fired from *Sugar And Spice*. You…got him fired, Mom. What the hell?"

A warm breeze blew across the cemetery, rattling the leaves on the trees. She got to her feet and stretched her hands above her head. Was this it? Was she suffering a mental breakdown? Talking to her mom who'd been gone for months. *Damn it.*

"I'm just so…I'm mad at you, Mom. And you're not even here for me to yell at you. I'm mad at you and it's not fair." She looked to the sky, her hands balled into fists at her sides. She took a deep breath and yelled, "It's not fair!"

The words burst out of her and floated out into the silent graveyard. She'd kept it all bottled up for too long. She'd tried to just shake it off while the anger and hurt rotted in her belly. Denial wasn't working anymore. It felt so damn good to let it out. To just say the actual words. Loudly. It felt so good she did it again.

"It's not fucking fair!"

This time as she sent her words out into the universe they were met by a distinct "tsk tsk," from the direction of the paved walkway winding through the grounds.

Elle snapped her head in the direction of the disapproval and saw a little old lady shaking her head and hurrying away from the wild woman cursing on her mother's grave. *Oh, great.*

"I'm sorry, ma'am," Elle called as embarrassed heat rushed up her neck into her cheeks. She was behaving so badly in such a reverent place. A place that demanded solemn, silent respect. The woman looked disgusted by her emotional outburst. Her need to expel the bad feelings had welled up inside her for too long and finally burst out of her in a totally inappropriate way. It was absolutely…hilarious. The laughter bubbled from deep inside her before she could stop it. "I didn't mean to offend you," she called out between guffaws. "I'm grieving!"

The old woman refused to make eye contact but swatted a hand in her direction as she shuffled off. The sight made Elle laugh even harder. Tears rolled down her cheeks until she was actually crying. It was too much. Her mother's secret was a betrayal, and it made her burn with anger. Suddenly the tears weren't funny and she gulped for breath and dropped to her knees, openly sobbing. Letting the emotion out in a whole different way.

When she had nothing left to choke out and she had finally caught her breath again, she shoved her hair out of her eyes and sat back on her heels, turning her face to the sun. She blew out a deep breath and for the first time in a long while, felt peaceful. She took her time getting to her feet, not wanting to lose the calm sensation. Overhead a flight of mourning doves dipped and circled before soaring off into the distance. The grounds were silent once again, and Elle felt like she was waking from a long slumber—a little fuzzy around the edges, but ready to face a new day.

She dusted herself off and looked around to see if anyone else had witnessed her moment, but she was alone. The old lady was long gone. Elle was ready to go home, but first she turned to the headstone again. "I love you, Mom. I'm still mad at you. But I love you."

As she entered her house, Elle tossed her keys into the bowl on the little table beside the front door. The blue Post-it note that simply said, "With Benji. Back for dinner," explained the silence. No matter. It would give her time to sort out her feelings. Yelling at her mother's grave had helped, but she was still carrying the weight of running out on Ashley.

She kicked off her shoes and collapsed onto the overstuffed recliner. How had she managed to make such a mess of everything? She'd screwed up her chance at having a relationship, she'd fucked up her chances on *Cook Off*, and worst of all, she'd hurt Ashley. She squeezed her eyes shut hoping she could push off the headache settling in. Not eating all day had been a mistake.

The knock on the door startled her out of her self-pity party. She didn't get up to answer it right away. Luci wouldn't knock. Neither would Marigold. Benji was with Luci, so it couldn't be him. But when the knocker didn't give up, she pushed up out of the recliner.

"Okay, okay. I'm coming."

"Well, hurry up. This tray is heavy," a familiar voice said through the door.

"Ashley?" Elle peered through the peephole before yanking the door open. "What the hell?"

"It's cannoli." Ashley thrust the tray into Elle's hands and pushed past her into the living room. "I thought you could use a little taste of heaven."

Elle held the tray tightly in her hands and blinked after Ashley, making herself at home on the sofa. Was this for real? Ashley had made cannoli for her and brought it to her house. On the same day she was crowned *Celebrity Cook Off* Champion and even though Elle had been acting like a total fool. Damn, the cannoli smelled good.

Elle inched closer to the sofa, unsure what to do with the tray of cannoli while Ashley toed off her flower-print Adidas and propped her feet up on the coffee table. "What is happening right here?"

"I told you," Ashley said, crossing her ankles, easy as could be. Like she didn't have a care in the world. "I brought you cannoli."

"But I've been so—"

"Oh yeah." Ashley nodded. "You've been a real piece of work. You're obviously going through something, so I thought making your favorite dessert was a small kindness I could do for you that might help. By the way, you might want to grab us some plates or at least napkins. I filled them right before I left the house, but they won't stay fresh forever and your arms must be getting tired holding that tray. It's Crate & Barrel, so it's heavy even when it's empty."

It *was* heavy, and Elle's stomach was starting to rumble from hunger. And this take charge, bossy version of Ashley was... damn sexy. She bumped some things out of the way on the coffee table, set the tray down, and grabbed some plates from the kitchen. She wasn't sure how she was lucky enough warrant this when what she deserved was to be kicked to the curb, but she wasn't going to waste this second chance.

As Elle sat down on the sofa, Ashley pulled the foil off the tray. "So. You sure scooted out of the studio quickly today. Again."

Right, bonehead. She hadn't even congratulated Ashley for her win. "Oh my God. Ash! You were awesome today and I'm so happy for you."

"Thanks. It felt awesome," she said, reaching for one of the sweet treats. "But, honestly, it would've felt a lot better to celebrate with you after the show."

Elle had been reaching for one of the flaky cannoli too but stopped mid-grab. Her stomach flopped with regret. "I know, I'm sorry. I just..." She shook her head. The only way to deal with this was honestly. She'd been honest with Mari about it, and honest at her mother's grave about it, but she hadn't been honest with the one person who most deserved an honest explanation. "I've been struggling since I found out my mom was the one who told the producers of *Sugar and Spice* about me and Josh. And then that stupid gossip rag story came out exposing it all and I was so afraid that I would drag you down with me. I felt like history was repeating itself. It was like I was cursed—sleep with me and fuck up your television career. It freaked me out."

Ashley didn't say anything, just took Elle's hand and gave it an encouraging squeeze.

Elle continued, "I thought I was protecting you. I didn't want to hurt you, but I ended up doing exactly that. Then I thought I could make it up to you when I showed up for filming today. I was rooting for you the whole time and, Ash, you were brilliant. When Freddie announced you were the champion...I was so damn proud. Everyone was cheering for you, and there I was, I'd been such an ass shutting you out the way I did. I knew you deserved better—someone better than me. So, I ran again, and I hurt you again. And, Ash, I'm so sorry."

Ashley nodded. Her eyes were teary, but not angry, just sad. "So, stop running."

"What?"

"Stop running and let me be your person. Ashley swung her feet down from the coffee table and turned to face her. If there's something freaking you out, you don't shut out your girlfriend. You let her help you through it. Let me help you through it."

"I want you to be my person and I want to be yours." Elle thought she was all cried out after her mini breakdown in the cemetery, but she was wrong. She swiped at her eyes with the back of her hand and looked at the beautiful woman beside her. Elle had acted appallingly, but Ashley was treating her with grace. "After all the stupid things I've done, you came here with my favorite dessert to take care of me?"

"I did." Ashley nodded scooting closer. A bit of powdered sugar from the cannoli was left on her upper lip. Elle wanted to kiss it off. "I love you."

"I love you too, Ash," she said. Her chest was full of love and the berry scent of Ashley's lip gloss was so tantalizing, Elle couldn't resist being drawn to them. "I'm going to kiss you now."

"You better." Ashley grinned. "I've been waiting for this for five days."

"Then I guess I better make it worth that wait." She slid onto the couch and took Ashley in her arms. Her body had missed the familiar warmth of being pressed to her. It was like a hunger. She drank in Ashley's scent, the magnolia of her shampoo. The emotion that washed over her was the definition of heaven on earth. Even more heavenly than cannoli. Ashley had started out as an acquired taste—a rival from Elle's past who appeared to have a drastically different world view based on the trophy wife lifestyle portrayed on her reality show, but now Elle couldn't get enough of her. She kissed Ashley greedily—lips mashing, teeth bumping. Fulfilling a deep need. She adored her.

Ashley sank back into the couch cushions, causing her dessert to drift dangerously from one edge of the plate to the other. "You're going to make me lose my cannoli."

"Screw the cannoli, delicious as they are…" Elle said, transferring the plate from Ashley's hand to the coffee table. In a smooth-as-silk move she straddled Ashley's lap, cupped her beautiful face in her palms, and resumed kissing her like she'd never stopped. Kissing Ashley felt so natural, so perfectly perfect that sometimes she thought once she started she might never stop.

Ashley's hands were on Elle's hips, then tickling up her spine, then in her hair. They were all over her. Heat pooled between Elle's legs. Her stomach tensed with excitement like she was on a roller coaster. A thrill ride. That's what Ashley's touch did to her.

"I want this off you." Ashley tugged at Elle's shirt and pulled it all the way off. Her gaze settled on Elle's breasts and she licked her lips. Apparently Elle wasn't the only one who was hungry for this.

"Then I want this off you." Elle slipped her hands under Ashley's paisley blouse. "What's that phrase you use? Tit for tat. Or, tit for tit, in this case."

"Eleanor, shut up and kiss me again," Ashley demanded against her mouth.

Elle nipped at Ashley's bottom lip, holding it between her teeth and giving it a tug. "Mmm. Okay." She slid off the couch to stand. She offered Ashley her hand.

Ashley's brows scrunched together in confusion. "What are you doing?"

"I'm pulling you off the couch, taking you upstairs. I'd like to fuck you with my strap-on."

Her eyes went wide, but then Ashley took her hand and hopped to her feet. "Lead the way."

They took the steps two at a time, kissing and touching each other along the way until finally Elle laid Ashley down on the bed before her. She helped shimmy off Ashley's white denim capris and panties and swapped her own jeans for her strap.

She stood at the edge of the bed and rubbed her hands along the creamy skin of Ashley's inner thighs, resting the dildo teasingly against her pussy. Ashley squirmed in front of her on the bed, her eyelids heavy with lust, a soft smile gracing her lips. Anticipation buzzed between them like an electrical current.

Elle brushed her thumb along Ashley's slit, turned on by the wetness she found there. "Are you ready for me?"

Ashley moaned, "Yes." She grabbed Elle's hips and pulled her in between her legs, emphasizing her response. She lay back again as Elle positioned the dildo to enter her. Ashley's legs wrapped around Elle's hips and a burst of excitement erupted in Elle's core. As heat rose within her, she rocked her hips along with the rhythm Ashley set. She didn't always orgasm while wearing a strap, but between being wrapped in Ashley's long, tanned legs, and the sexy way Ashley bit her bottom lip while her eyes rolled with pleasure, the likelihood of it was greatly improved.

As Ashley's blissful moans made it clear she was moving closer to tipping over the edge of pleasure, Elle increased the pace of her thrusts. She wanted so badly to witness this beautiful woman come undone. Pressure built between her own legs as Ashley finally cried out with release.

"Oh my God, baby," Ashley growled, and gripped the sheets as the orgasm rocked her body. Her legs fell over the side of the bed as she sucked air, recovering. Faster than Elle would've expected, Ashley sat up and unbuckled the strap. She pulled Elle onto the bed. "I can't wait another minute to taste you."

Elle held eye contact as Ashley slid down her until that last moment when Ashley's head was buried between her legs. She tangled her hands in Ashley's golden hair and let herself get lost in the pleasure Ashley's tongue provided as it circled and stroked. The excitement that had been building inside her from fucking Ashley was sweeping her quickly toward a crescendo. The edges of real life around her went fuzzy as the first wave of her orgasm washed over her.

Ashley didn't stop until Elle's final shudders and aftershocks subsided. Only then did she crawl back up next to Elle and kiss her squarely on the mouth.

Elle wrapped her arms around her and deepened the kiss. She didn't know how it had happened, but she knew something very, very good had come into her life, and as far as she was concerned, she was never going to let go of her again.

CHAPTER TWENTY-FIVE

Ashley stood watch over the flank steak sizzling on her backyard grill. She was re-creating her competition-winning meal for Elle, Luci, and Benji. This time she felt much calmer with home-court advantage.

"I can't believe you won't let me do anything." Elle sat on the edge of the inground pool, legs dangling in the water while the teenagers splashed around in the far end. "I'm not used to someone else being the cook. I don't know what to do with myself."

"It's like a *Freaky Friday* situation," she laughed. "You're the one lounging poolside while I'm the one rustling up the grub. It *is* a little weird."

"We should put those two to work." Elle tipped her head in the direction of the teens. "I think they're having too much fun."

Ashley smiled and gazed across the pool as Luci tossed a neon-pink beach ball to Benji who made an overly dramatic dive to catch it. Inviting them all over for a little pool party had been a great idea—things at the Castle house had been much too quiet the past few weeks. Having kids splashing in the pool really livened things up.

"Let them enjoy the carefree time together," she said, flipping the steak with a long set of tongs like a grilling pro. "It's puppy love. It's sweet."

Elle stood and adjusted the sarong tied around her waist over her swimsuit. Her shoulders were sun-kissed pink and as she raised the umbrella over the dining table on the patio, Ashley's gaze was drawn to Elle's shapely arms. "Calling it a cute name doesn't make me feel any better about how smitten those two seem to be." She put a gentle hand on Ashley's shoulder and gave it a squeeze as she changed the subject. "Are you nervous about tomorrow?"

"No. I mean, kind of." Ashley had spent the better part of the day trying not to think about her meeting tomorrow with the people at Eats! Channel. She was prepared, and that was enough. She didn't want to trip over the line into obsessive worry about what she would say and do and whether or not the network would support her book idea. The pool party had served as a wonderful distraction up to this point. "Do you think I got too full of myself with the *Queen of the Castle* stuff and I'm shooting too high going for the book too?"

She still couldn't believe Jill had managed to negotiate the changes she wanted for the next season of the show—the final season. The focus would switch to Ashley putting the house on the market and finding a fresh start in a new home that was just hers. It would show her moving on. David would make appearances as his filming schedule allowed. She was ending the show on her terms. But as her agent had so sagely said when she told Ashley the good news, that was just good Hollywood luck. It came your way when you spent your summer hiatus winning a cooking contest.

"Absolutely not." Elle was incredulous. "You deserve to have it all. I want you to have it all."

Ashley took a break from broccoli florets on the grill and turned to Elle. This gorgeous, confident woman had come into her life like a whirlwind, shaken things up, shared her kitchen and her bed, and was now standing in front of her declaring that she wanted her to have it all. "You are amazing, and I am the luckiest woman on the planet." She punctuated the statement with a sweet kiss on Elle's rosy lips. Elle tasted like chlorine, and her smile pressing against Ashley's mouth made her feel like she could take on the world.

"The luckiest woman in the world knows better than to turn her back on the grill, right?" Elle teased. "That oiled-up broccoli singes easily."

"I know what I'm doing. In case you haven't heard, I'm the *Celebrity Cook Off* Champion." She gave it right back. She turned her attention to the grill, but she kept talking over her shoulder. "Are you sure you don't want to come to the meeting with me tomorrow? You're a vital part of the book project. I can't do it without you."

"First of all, you totally *can* do it without me," Elle said as she uncorked a bottle of wine. "I will do anything you ask to make this project a success. I'm on board one hundred percent, but this is your pitch to make. I will be cheering you on from the wings, but you're the star. You got this."

Ashley took a sip of wine and pulled dinner off the grill. The steak had near perfect char lines, and the aroma was a heavenly mix of savory beef and smoke. Although the steak needed to rest, she was excited to slice it up and serve the meal to her guests, and that was a feeling she had never experienced before. It had been a long five weeks waiting out the fate of *Queen of the Castle*, but she'd spent those weeks wisely. She'd learned how to cook, she'd not only had her show renewed, but also convinced the producers to green light her vision for it. And most importantly, she'd found an inner strength that she didn't know she had. Yes, she was definitely ready for the book pitch meeting. *I got this!*

CHAPTER TWENTY-SIX

Ashley stood in the large conference room and marveled at her surroundings. The large windows overlooking the lots below and the formal mahogany table were so different from sets where she usually spent time when she was at the studios. When you were mingling with the executives, the view was a bit higher brow. She got to the point, wrapping up her presentation, summoning every last ounce of moxie to bring the proposal home.

"So that's the idea, a book of Elle's family recipes and my home-improvement projects, interspersed with personal stories from Elle and me. The pages in the folder in front of you provide a sample of the writing style and, of course, the stats from Elle's Instagram speak for themselves. I'm happy to address any questions you might have now." Out of the corner of her eye Ashley caught Jill's encouraging nod. The pitch had gone exactly as practiced.

But though Producer Kelly and the Eats! Channel executives were politely thumbing through her informational packet, their expressions remained stone cold. They weren't completely sold on the project.

Beside her, Jill sat with a confident, yet pleasant smile, patiently waiting for the other side of the table to speak first. Ashley crossed her legs and tried to fix her face into the same expression. Jill had reminded her that showing you were comfortable during the silences could speak volumes about your confidence in the project. Ashley hoped that was what she and Jill were doing, because it was killing her to bite her tongue and not give one final push for the book.

Finally, the Suit sitting in the buttery leather swivel chair next to Producer Kelly spoke. "Ms. Castle, we loved the chemistry you and Ms. Bissett had on *Celebrity Cook Off.* The episode where your pasta got dumped and she came to your rescue—"

"I'm sorry about that. We didn't mean to break the rules," Ashley interrupted him, unable to hold back her thoughts any longer. That stupid mistake cost Elle her spot in the finals. She couldn't let it screw up this too. She had to apologize, or explain, or do *something*. "I mean, we meant to do what we did. We just didn't know we were breaking the rules. I would've never used her dough if I'd known it was a violation or whatever."

The tight-lipped, wide-eyed stare Jill had fixed on her made Ashley clam up again.

"Why don't you let Mr. Pierce finish?" The sweet smile returned to Jill's lips. Her eyes narrowed though like they were pinning Ashley in place.

Ashley swallowed down her excitement and nodded politely. "Of course."

"Ms. Castle, I'm going to level with you." The Suit clasped his hands in front of him on the conference table. Was he praying? Bracing himself in case she flipped out? *Oh, God, what?* "A book isn't exactly what we had in mind for either you or Ms. Bissett."

Ashley's heart sunk. She'd blown it.

CHAPTER TWENTY-SEVEN

"He actually said that?" Elle was literally on the edge of her seat, in this case the sofa in her living room, her knees bumping up against the coffee table as Ashley rehashed her meeting with the Eats! Channel executives. Luci sat on one side of her, mouth agape, hanging on every word. Marigold perched on the arm of the sofa on the opposite side, back straight, face calm as if absorbing the words before reacting.

Across from them all, Ashley sat in the plush armchair, glass of wine in one hand leaving the other free to gesture wildly along with her tale. "Yes! Then he said, 'A book isn't exactly what we had in mind for either you or Ms. Bissett.' I about died on the spot!"

"God, you were using formal names," Elle cracked. "Too bad I missed this meeting live and in person."

"I know. It was completely nerve-wracking." Ashley's eyes widened as she nodded. She paused and took a sip of wine. It seemed to pull her back to the story. "I was so embarrassed that I'd blurted out that awkward apology, and then he said *that*...I was ready to grab my purse and be shown the door. But then he said the good part."

"The good part!" Luci bounced in her seat like a teenaged Tigger. "What was the good part?"

"He said they wanted to give us a television show. You and me, and our 'chemistry.' Hour-long episodes based on the material and recipes we planned to use for the book. The book will still be published, and we would market it along our own line of cookware and crockery."

"Crockery?" Luci guffawed. "That sounds so old-timey."

"Our own damn line of dishes? Get outta here." Elle placed a hand on her daughter's knee. She needed to focus and the ball of excitement bouncing next to her was making that tough. It might be time to cut the Mountain Dew out of Luci's diet again. "Let me get this straight. They want to give us—you and me— our own show? Because of the book idea?"

"Not exactly because of the book." Ashley's shoulders hunched in a sheepish shrug. "More because we have that chemistry—the kind that makes television magic happen and also because the test viewers who screened *Celebrity Cook Off* indicated they would watch more of us."

"Mmmhmm." Elle had been in the business long enough to know that wasn't the full scoop. "What's the catch?"

"It's not a catch, per se." Ashley paused and bit her bottom lip and batted her eyes just the tiniest bit. Making herself look sweet like the spoonful of sugar to help the medicine go down. "But we will have to appear in commercials for the cookware."

Commercials? Elle's stomach gave a reflexive squeeze, but that excited sparkle in Ashley's eyes eased her back off the ledge. Like everything would be okay if they were in this adventure together.

"I'm gonna stop you right there," Marigold said as she stood. "The commercials are a deal-breaker. Elle hasn't done them since she was a little kid and she's not going to start again now. But thank you for considering her for this."

Elle knew Mari was just doing her usual agent thing, but she saw the way Ashley's face fell when she said, "deal-breaker."

The book was so important to her and then she got the added thrill of being offered a show on Eats! Channel, only for it all to be taken away because of Elle's no-commercials rule. She was responsible for that heartbroken look on the face of the woman she loved. Yes, *loved* was the right word. Her chest felt heavy as she saw tears glistening in Ashley's eyes. Stupid no-commercials rule. It wasn't even her rule. It was one that her mother had insisted upon after Elle scored the role on *Sugar and Spice*. Another one of her mother's great management moves. Only this time there was something she could do about it. Her mom hadn't been right about other decisions as a manager. Maybe she'd been wrong about the no-commercials rule too. Maybe doing a few commercials wasn't such a big deal.

"Hold on a sec," she said, holding her open hands up in the air as if casting a magic spell to freeze everyone in place. "Commercials don't have to be a deal-breaker."

Marigold and Luci shared a look that said they both thought the real Elle may have been replaced by a pod person from *Invasion of the Body Snatchers*.

"Elle, are you sure about this?" Marigold's tone was overly gentle like she was afraid of this pod person who was volunteering to do commercial work. "No commercials has been your mantra since the day I met you, and now—"

"Now I think it's time for a change," Elle said firmly. "That was my *mom's* rule for my career, and it turns out she might not have been right about absolutely everything."

In two strides, Ashley was out of her chair and beside Elle on the couch. Her previously crushed expression had shifted—her chin was out, her shoulders back—she took Elle's hand and held on tightly. Her mood had shifted completely into protective mode. "Elle, I don't want you to do something that will take your career off the track you've set for it. I wasn't thinking when I agreed to the commercials. I'm so sorry. We can go back and ask them if they'll just take the book. Who knows? They might take it. They could release it after *Cook Off* airs, make a few extra bucks."

Marigold nodded in agreement and started tapping notes into her phone. "I'll talk to Jill. We can put together a package for a counteroffer, take it back to Eats! Channel and work something out. This is not a problem."

Elle looked at Ashley, her big blue eyes so full of love, willing to give up the project for which she'd worked so damn hard. Elle knew in that instant she would do anything for this woman. "No. It's not a problem at all and you don't have to take anything back to the Eats! Channel. This project is important to Ashley and it's important to me. Why would I let doing a few commercials stand in the way of that? I want to do this. I'm all in."

"All in," Ashley repeated as a smile brightened her worried face. "Me too."

"Ash." Elle shifted on the couch and their knees bumped together. "I love you and I can't wait for what comes next for us."

"I love you too," Ashley said and leaned in for a tender kiss that sent shivers all through Elle.

"Mom. Mom!" Luci squealed and poked at Elle's shoulder. "Mari and I are still in the room, you know."

Ashley's laughter against Elle's lips was like heaven, but they broke off the kiss in deference to the others in the room.

"We'll continue this later," she whispered to Ashley before addressing the room. "We're writing a book *and* making a television show. Let's celebrate!"

ONE YEAR LATER

Elle looked in the mirror and picked at a clump of mascara on her lashes. Damn mascara, she hated the stuff. But the professional who did her makeup had insisted on it. Despite the clump, she couldn't hold back her goofy grin.

Things had turned out pretty damn well since her *Celebrity Cook Off* appearance. *Doing It All With Ashley and Elle* was a hit after the first season, and they were getting ready to start filming a second. Luci had just finished her high school sophomore year, was still heavily into surfing, and officially dating YouTube sensation Benji Daniels. And Elle and Ashley...their renewed success suited them just fine. They were going as strongly as ever.

"Stop fussing with your makeup! You look perfect," Marigold scolded, squeezing into the little dressing room and quietly shutting the door behind her. "Are you ready for this? Do you know what you're going to say and everything?"

Elle blew out a big breath. This wasn't the time to let her nerves get to her. She was more than ready. "It's a semi-scripted situation. There will be prompts."

"No, I know." Marigold scooted out of the way as Elle pushed her chair back and stood. "Are you nervous?"

That wasn't quite what she was feeling. There was hope fluttering in her heart, and joy welled up in her chest. She was a hodgepodge of emotions, but they were all positive. "I'm excited."

"Then let's do this."

They opened the door to find Luci rushing down the hall. "Mom! Mom, Ashley's waiting for you." She grabbed Marigold's hand. "Aunt Mari, you come with me. I'll show you where we're supposed to stand."

Classic Luci—still as enthusiastic and bossy as ever. The two of them scurried down the hall whispering to each other. Elle took a moment to take another deep breath, running her hands down the front of her jacket. It was go time.

She found Ashley farther down the hall around the corner, waiting for her like Luci said, so they could face this crowd together.

Ashley's eyes lit up as their gazes met, her smile as bright and spectacular as the sun. Her hair was pulled into a knot at the back of her head, with a couple of loose strands framing her beautiful face. Her cream silk frock wasn't a traditional wedding dress, but it was floaty and ethereal, and gathered at the side of her waist making her look like a goddess. She *was* a freaking goddess. Elle's chest was so full of love, she thought it might burst.

"Love, you look absolutely stunning." She stepped into Ashley's open arms.

"So do you."

Their lips met in a delicious kiss that sent a jolt of pleasure through Elle. "Mmm. I could do this all day."

"Me too," Ashley whispered. "But we have a wedding to attend."

Elle took her hand and stared into those sparkling blue eyes. "I love you, Ashley Castle."

"I love you, Elle Bissett." Ashley grinned back. "Let's go get married."

Hand in hand they pushed through the doors of the chapel and walked down the aisle to do just that.

Bella Books, Inc.
Women. Books. Even Better Together.
P.O. Box 10543
Tallahassee, FL 32302
Phone: (800) 729-4992
www.BellaBooks.com

More Titles from Bella Books

Mabel and Everything After – Hannah Safren
978-1-64247-390-2 I 274 pgs I paperback: $17.95 I eBook: $9.99
A law student and a wannabe brewery owner find that the path to a
fairy tale happily-ever-after is often the long and scenic route.

To Be With You – TJ O'Shea
978-1-64247-419-0 I 348 pgs I paperback: $19.95 I eBook: $9.99
Sometimes the choice is between loving safely or loving bravely.

I Dare You to Love Me – Lori G. Matthews
978-1-64247-389-6 I 292 pgs I paperback: $18.95 I eBook: $9.99
An enemy-to-lovers romance about daring to follow your heart, even
when it's the hardest thing to do.

The Lady Adventurers Club - Karen Frost
978-1-64247-414-5 I 300 pgs I paperback: $18.95 I eBook: $9.99
Four women. One undiscovered Egyptian tomb. One (maybe) angry
Egyptian goddess. What could possibly go wrong?

Golden Hour - Kat Jackson
978-1-64247-397-1 I 250 pgs I paperback: $17.95 I eBook: $9.99
Life would be so much easier if Lina were afraid of something
basic—like spiders—instead of something significant. Something like
real, true, healthy love.

Schuss – E. J. Noyes
978-1-64247-430-5 I 276 pgs I paperback: $17.95 I eBook: $9.99
They're best friends who both want something more, but what if
admitting it ruins the best friendship either of them have had?